WHITE SLEEPER

A Novel

David R. Fett
&
Stephen Langford

Synergy Books

White Sleeper
Published by Synergy Books
P.O. Box 30071
Austin, Texas 78755

For more information about our books, please write us, e-mail us at info@synergybooks.net, or visit our web site at www.synergybooks.net.

Publisher's Cataloging-in-Publication
(Provided by Quality Books, Inc.)

Fett, David.
White sleeper : a novel / David Fett and Stephen Langford.
p. cm.
LCCN 2010927334
ISBN-13: 9780984504022
ISBN-10: 0984504028

1. Physicians--Fiction. 2. United States. Federal Bureau of Investigation--Officials and employees--Fiction. 3. Centers for Disease Control and Prevention (U.S.)--Fiction. 4. White supremacy movements--United States--Fiction. 5. Communicable diseases--Arkansas--Fiction. 6. Arkansas--Fiction. I. Langford, Stephen, 1958- II. Title.

PS3606.E82W45 2010 813'.6
QBI10-600101

This is a work of fiction. All of the characters and events portrayed in this book are fictional, and any resemblance to real people or incidents is purely coincidental.

10 9 8 7 6 5 4 3 2 1

PART ONE

. . . . . .

DARK BEGINNINGS

CHAPTER 1

1996

The cadre of black ATF Yukons was spread under a pair of white pines overlooking the wide, rushing Salmon River. The river was also referred to as the River of No Return. Most locals didn't know the story behind the alternate moniker, but names were a peculiar thing in Idaho. Back in the 1800s, when Congress was considering making it a state, a lobbyist named George Willing suggested the Indian name Idaho. It stuck, but it was later discovered that the name was a prank by Mr. Willing. The word "Idaho" had no meaning. Mr. Willing, however, sealed his place in history by providing the only state name that meant absolutely nothing.

This tidbit compromised most of what special agent in charge Ryan Conley, a thirty-four-year-old, prematurely gray ATF agent, knew about Idaho. He zipped up his thin ATF jacket and took a deep breath of the crisp mountain air.

Retiring to Idaho was an attractive idea to him, considering he was based out of Los Angeles where fresh air was at a premium. He watched the river's cascade of rushing water. Nature always had a hypnotic effect on Conley.

Agent Wendy Berkey, a thin, pretty blonde who was, as usual, chain smoking Marlboros, drew his attention away from the river.

"Everyone's in position," she said.

"Tell them to wait for my signal to move in."

"You got it."

Wendy strode away. Conley watched as she quietly filled in the others. They hung on her every word, only occasionally glancing toward Conley. Conley couldn't help but smile. This was his first outing as the special agent in charge, and it was about time; he had been stuck at the same pay grade for five years. A buddy had wisely advised him that if he wanted to move up the ladder, things had to change. At first, Conley was discouraged. He wasn't good at political gamesmanship. Conley was, plain and simple, a law enforcement officer. He was a serious agent who did his job well, but nothing more. But his failure to advance weighed heavily on him. He didn't know how to pull himself out of his rut—or his five-by-five cubicle.

His luck had changed with the publication of the cop thriller *Wasteland*, which was written by fellow ATF agent Mark Summers, whose workstation was opposite Conley's. After the book hit the stands and the movie rights were snapped up a few weeks later, Summers had become an instant celebrity, and the never-ending payday from his book made his weekly ATF paycheck unnecessary. Summers gave notice one morning, and by that afternoon, all his files were deposited on the nearest desk: Agent Conley's. At first Conley was furious at having so many cases dumped on him, but then he ran across the file of Harlan Justice Curran.

Curran was an anti-government white supremacist who treasured his own twisted beliefs over the principles of the

United States Constitution. It dawned on Agent Conley that lady luck had finally shined upon him. This was the opportunity he had been hoping for. If he tracked down, captured, and prosecuted Curran, he was sure to advance within the agency. Summers had done all the legwork, and all Conley had to do was take the credit.

Conley had looked around, hoping no one was watching him as he examined the file. He had leaned back in his chair, trying to appear casual. Curran had fallen into his lap and he was going take the ball into the end zone.

At the next week's staff meeting, Conley had brought up Curran. He described what a threat Curran was and explained that there was solid evidence that he had been involved in the murder of a pair of ATF agents in 1994. Naturally, his superiors couldn't deny him the resources he requested. Conley had whipped everyone into a frenzy. He sold everyone on the idea that Curran was the devil incarnate, and the ATF was going to smite him and send him back to hell.

As the months went by, Conley referred to Summers's footwork as his own. He gave the information out piecemeal, which made him look like a boy wonder. Conley never felt guilty for riding on Summers's work. Summers's book was enjoying its fifteenth week on the *New York Times* bestseller list. He sincerely doubted whether Summers remembered the ATF or that he'd even been an agent.

When *Wasteland* hit its eighteenth week on the *New York Times* bestseller list, ATF received a reliable tip on Curran's location. A gunrunner, facing a weapons charge, traded Curran's address in Idaho for an easy one-year stretch in San Quentin. Conley was rewarded with special-agent-in-charge status and a ticket to Idaho with a handpicked tactical team.

Conley signaled to Wendy, who nodded and whispered to the others. They began their stealthy sweep toward the Curran cabin, a mere half mile away. Conley hid behind a white pine tree and brought a pair of binoculars up to his eyes. The paint had long since faded on the modest cabin, and the roof was in dire need of repair. The front door popped open, and a boy of about sixteen came out with his nose in a book. A black Labrador followed him, urinated too close to the house, and then scurried back inside. Conley dropped the binoculars and hoped this wouldn't get messy.

CHAPTER 2

Harlan Curran finished his eggs and bacon. He sat back in his chair, patting his stomach and watching his wife Peggy clear the dishes as she had done for the last twenty years. Harlan was fifty-three but looked to be in his late sixties. He had a silver-gray mane of hair but a brown mustache.

Harlan loved his plot of land because he didn't have to see the cancer that had spread across his great country. Jews, blacks, and Hispanics were consuming his once wonderful America. They had high offices, and they were on TV giving him the news the way they saw it. Twenty years ago, he decided he'd had enough, and he joined the Knights of the White Order to set America back on its rightful course. Whites had taken America from the Indians and had made it into the might of the world. Now the invaders were trying to destroy all he loved.

All Harlan's hopes for the future had been tied up in his son, Ben, since he was old enough to talk. "The Knights of The White Order will cleanse America of the poison in her heart. If we're effective, the federal government will have to listen," Harlan told his son. But as time went on, the feds didn't listen; they didn't see the threat. The Knights of The White Order knew they had to strike. And they did. They killed two undercover ATF agents in 1994 and robbed several banks in Illinois to finance their operations.

Harlan had come into the order as merely a soldier for the cause, but now, twenty-odd years later, he was one of its presumptive leaders. General Curran was his unofficial title, and his leadership had made him a federal target.

Harlan pushed his chair back from the kitchen table. He sipped a cup of instant coffee and stood in the doorway, looking out over his land. He never tired of the fresh air and the breeze that gently swayed his precious white pines. It was a perfect picture. Nothing had changed on his land in fifty years.

As he looked toward the Salmon River, he remembered he'd been meaning to take Ben fishing. The steelhead were running hard. It would be good father-son time. They'd fish and he'd tell Ben stories his father had told him. And it didn't matter if they didn't catch anything—that wasn't the point. He was Ben's father, and he wanted Ben to be prepared for the real world. He wanted to tell him that the white race was the superior race and that's the way God had intended it. "If you ain't white, you ain't right"—that's what he needed to pound into Ben's skull.

He saw Ben pull a paperback book out his back pocket and watched him. Harlan was glad Ben was a good reader; he just had to be careful what he read. His son would regularly zip through a book on a weekend. Ben was very bright, and Harlan often wondered what his IQ was. He wasn't sure where Ben's intellect came from. Harlan didn't consider himself a genius, but it was clear his son was exceptional.

Harlan whistled through his teeth to get Ben's attention. Ben snapped around and smiled broadly.

"Ben, you wanna go fishing tomorrow?" Harlan asked.

Ben nodded eagerly. "Yeah, but we'll need bait, Dad."

Harlan looked down, kicking a mound of dirt with his boot. He walked up to Ben and put his hands on his son's shoulders.

"How about we make a quick trip later this afternoon?" Harlan said. Ben beamed and scurried off to the shed to get the fishing poles and check the lines to make sure they were in good shape. It had been awhile since they'd been fishing, and he wanted to make sure all was in working order. Harlan followed him and reminded him to use his favorite lure.

"I hope she hasn't thrown it out," Ben said.

"She does have a habit of doing that." Harlan's wife hated clutter. It was a constant war between them since he was a pack rat. Harlan and Ben saw Peggy hanging the laundry on a line.

"Mom, have you seen my grand sweetie lure?" Peggy's brow furrowed in the way it always did when she was asked a question she didn't know the answer to.

"What in the Sam Hill is a grand sweetie lure? Please speak to me in English, Ben." Ben tried to explain, but Peggy just looked more puzzled. "I've got to do laundry, Ben. I don't have time for this nonsense."

Harlan put his arm around Ben and winked at him. "It'll take longer to explain it to your mother than just going to find it yourself." Ben nodded, and Harlan headed into the house. He stopped to look back at his family in the doorway, taking in the peaceful scene.

The bullet that Tom Griffard—the brand new ATF sharpshooter—fired traveled a half mile in less than two seconds. Peggy was about to tell Ben to look for his lure in the garage when the bullet silenced her. Ben looked on in quaking horror as the drying sheets were spattered with blood. Peggy's thick body collapsed in an instant. Ben was freckled with blood.

"Mom!" Ben cried in a terrible, earth-shattering scream. Harlan grabbed his son and shoved him toward the cabin.

Griffard lined up his scope with Ben in his crosshairs. He had another direct head shot, but the wind picked up and the sheet on the line blew his angle. He cursed and started sweeping the area for his next target, but he didn't get a chance—Conley's boot was in his face. Griffard's rifle fell to the side.

"What the hell are you doing, Griffard?"

Griffard looked up at him innocently, as though nothing had happened. Conley noticed there was something wrong in his eyes. How could this have happened on his watch? Conley flashed to Griffard's file. He remembered registering a gap in service. Griffard had been a top-notch marksman in the army, but there was nothing in the file to cover the time between his army service and his arrival at the ATF. Conley had been about to look into it when he was distracted by a crisis between two colleagues. When he returned to his desk, he closed the file and put it on the pile that contained files of the other agents he had chosen for his team; he had never inquired further. Had he dropped the ball?

Now, Griffard had just shot an unarmed woman, and on Conley's watch.

"You shot the mother," Conley said, hoping Griffard's blank eyes would register shock or perhaps remorse.

"It was a bitch of a shot, but it came off well, don't you think?" Griffard said.

It was far worse than he thought. Conley moved toward Griffard and was apoplectic. He had made a horrible mistake hiring Griffard, and there was no way to fix the situation; the damage had been done.

"Did I give you the order to shoot?"

"It was a perfect shot. You should have seen it. I had to take it. Wait till you see it close up. It was a hard one, but I pulled it off. It was really sweet."

Griffard reached for his rifle, but Conley kicked it away.

"What are you? Some kind of head case?"

Griffard suddenly fell silent and looked away. He fidgeted with his hands, pressing them together in a kneading motion, smiled, and rocked ever so slightly. As he stared out into space, Conley watched and felt ill.

Ben and Harlan made it into the cabin, slamming the door behind them. Ben collapsed in a chair, shaking. Harlan grabbed his shoulders.

"We gotta avenge your mom, Son. This is it. Those bastards are out there waiting to kill us. If you ain't white, you ain't right." Ben broke into tears, and Harlan shook him.

"No time to cry, Ben. No time to cry."

Harlan released his son and marched over to the ammo locker. He unlocked the combination padlock that secured his arsenal of weapons: twelve-gauge shotguns, assorted hunting rifles, and an M-16.

"You gotta be strong for her. You got to do her proud."

"But we could get killed, Dad."

"Not before we take a few with us. Besides, we'll be in a better place, and we'll have the last laugh. They only let white Christians into heaven."

Harlan looked into Ben's eyes and could see his son understood. If they died, they'd be seeing Peggy soon.

Harlan loaded the M-16 and glimpsed out the window. He saw some movement several yards off and squeezed the trigger. He deftly fired clip after clip out the window, desperately fending off the ATF, and looked toward his son. Ben grabbed a hunting rifle and paused. Harlan smiled and nodded. Ben joined him at the window, took aim, and fired.

Agent Conley heard the first few shots from the cabin, and then his radio crackled. It was Wendy.

"How do we proceed?"

Conley's stomach was churning, but Griffard had committed him. Now he had no choice.

"Take down the cabin. I repeat, take down the cabin."

Conley clicked off his radio and heard his agents' Uzis and AK-47s returning fire. The gun battle raged, echoing through the River of No Return as Conley squatted a few hundred yards away, trying to regain his composure.

The crackling and popping sounded like the Fourth of July, but Conley was hardly humming "Stars and Stripes Forever." He was watching his career go down the drain. He sat behind a tree, at a safe distance, as the gun battle went on. He held on to Griffard's gun, so at least he could do no more damage. How many agents would he lose because of this maniac? There was nothing he could do. He had to wait it out. He wished the Harlan Curran file had never shown up on his desk. Conley rubbed the cross around his neck, silently praying that it would all work out. After all, he wasn't a bad guy. In fact, he was supposed to be one of the good guys. He just wanted to serve the people and protect the United States Constitution.

The first bullet that hit Harlan Curran pierced his hand and skipped through his shoulder. Ben heard the thump. He looked over at his dad who was staggering, dazed.

Ben saw the second bullet impact Harlan's cheek and blow out his lower teeth. They scattered over a credenza Peggy had picked up at a yard sale last year. The third bullet, and the fatal one, slammed into his chest and made a hole in his back the diameter of a soccer ball. Ben watched his father fall in a heap, gasping for air. The bullet had blown out a lung. Ben grabbed his dad and cradled him as he made his last bloody gasp. Harlan's eyes went dead. Ben shook him and shouted.

"Dad! Dad!" Ben's voice got shrill. "Dad!" But Harlan didn't answer. He just lay there as the eight pints of blood in his frame spilled out across the floor. Ben was the only one left now. There were no cousins, aunts, or uncles. The Curran line ended with him.

The ATF agents hadn't had a shot returned in over ten minutes. Wendy Berkey radioed Conley to advise him they were moving in. Conley told her to be careful.

The tactical team rushed the cabin and kicked in the door. The room was splattered in blood. In the center of all that carnage was Ben, who pointed and clicked an empty gun. The ATF agents grabbed the boy in mere seconds. They tried to pry the revolver from his hand, but the sheer anger and vengeance that consumed him wouldn't allow him to let go. He only let go of the empty Glock when Carl Donner, a thick bear of an agent, socked him in the jaw. Ben went limp.

When Conley surveyed the damage, he considered himself lucky. Two agents were wounded, and the suspect was dead. He had wished for the death of Harlan Justice Curran and got it. He thought he might still get his new pay grade and be able to build that sundeck his wife wanted on the house.

Conley stepped out of the cabin and saw Griffard alone and mumbling to himself. He fidgeted and kneaded his hands. Brief, terrifying smirks crept over his face as he looked at Peggy Curran's body. Conley was appalled and knew that somehow he'd have to deal with the Tom Griffard problem.

CHAPTER 3

1997

The steady silence of the hospital floor was broken by a pair of running footsteps. Dr. Root looked up from the charts he was reviewing. The great Dr. Paddock and his wife were running toward him carrying their daughter. Dr. Paddock was the chief of infectious diseases at UCLA. He was considered a god in his specialty. His wife Kim, usually cheerful, had dark circles under her eyes.

"She can't breathe," Kim said. Little Lacey Paddock was gasping for air. Paddock looked paralyzed, terrified.

"She's suffering from an ascending paralysis that has been working up her body since last night," Paddock said.

Root jumped into action to get Lacey intubated before she stopped breathing. The chief resident prayed he wouldn't make a mistake under Dr. Paddock's watchful, terrified eye.

If he slipped up with the daughter of the chief of infectious diseases, Root would be lucky to get a job in Tijuana.

Dr. Root was round and good-natured, with a laugh that might have annoyed strangers but delighted his friends. In many ways he was too nice to be chief resident. He had endured the heartlessness of numerous teachers over the years and swore he would break the chain of cruelty. Dr. Root was going to be the kinder and gentler chief resident and prove you could get the same results without having a temper tantrum every two minutes.

His annoying laugh had attracted Emily Cohen, a petite pharmacy sales rep that adored cuddly men. A quick courtship was followed by a marriage. Root felt lucky meeting Emily; it validated his cherished belief that being good-natured wasn't a bad thing. He met a great girl, and he was going to continue to be a good guy.

Root went into attack mode to find out what was paralyzing Lacey Paddock. *You have to go by the book*, he thought. He needed to pull it all together today. He ran a series of blood cultures, toxin screens, and a lumbar puncture. Were her white blood cells elevated? No. Had she been exposed to pesticides, organophosphates, Malathion? The answer was no. He pondered mercury or lead poisoning, but the answer was still no, and Lacey was getting worse. She was dying. Dr. Paddock was one of the top five doctors in the country in his specialty. How the hell was he, a thirty-three-year-old chief resident, going to diagnose something that Dr. Paddock couldn't figure out? Root used MRIs, CT scans, and every other tool available to him, but Lacey kept getting worse, and time was running out.

Paddock, wracked with grief, his eyes red from crying, kept close check on Root's progress. Root paged all the fellowship students in for help. This needed to be solved in the same way it was on TV—in an hour and in four acts—but that wasn't reality. The odds were they'd never find out what was killing Lacey until they did a postmortem.

The youthful doctors offered solutions but ultimately drew a blank when it came to finding the solution to the Lacey Paddock problem. Why was a healthy kid suddenly dying? There were no answers, and Root knew he was unlikely to find one.

Root made desperate calls around the country to other doctors. Some were former classmates, and others were the top in their fields. Charts were faxed and reviewed, but every possibility came to a dead end. There was no reason why this was happening to Lacey. Root, in a rare moment of recklessness, consulted a former medical student who had dropped out in favor of holistic medicine. But he got nothing.

Doctors had been coming in and out of Root's office with different theories, but three hours had passed since anyone had knocked at his door. Root felt like the walls of his compact office were closing in on him. He thought back to his internship at Mass General in Boston. The chief of surgery said the hardest part of their job was telling the loved ones the truth. Root had gotten better at giving bad news, but he'd never had to give it to someone he revered. He ratcheted up his courage to give the Paddocks the hopeless update that Lacey would probably die within twenty-four hours, and there was nothing he could do to save her.

CHAPTER 4

Dr. Dave Richards, a thirty-two-year-old fellow, felt a poke in his ribs. His eyes fluttered open and found nurse Nancy Mock staring down at him with a scornful glare. Nurse Mock didn't exactly have the kind of face you wanted to wake up to. She was easily a hundred pounds overweight and sported some hair on her upper lip that indicated a hormonal imbalance. But since she was by far the meanest nurse on the floor, no one dared mention to her the great recent advances in laser hair removal. Dave looked around and realized he had fallen asleep in an empty hospital room.

"Dr. Richards, I need this room," Nurse Mock said with her hands on her hips and her lips pursed. Dave had done a double shift the night before and figured he'd take a twenty-minute nap—but he never woke up.

"Dr. Richards, unless you're checking in, you gotta move."

"Take it easy, Nancy." Dave hopped off the bed.

"That's Nurse Mock," she said. Dave considered throwing out a smart-ass comment but knew it certainly wouldn't come to a good end. There'd be a meeting with the head nurse and Dr. Root, and he'd have to take a class where he'd have to swear to change his ways. Instead, Dave gave an insincere smile to Nurse Mock and headed out into the hallway.

Dave let out a groan as he stretched. He turned down another hallway and saw the coffee machine. He realized he had no change, so he'd have to turn on the charm at the nurses' station. Dave was just shy of six feet tall and slim. He didn't look like a doctor; he looked more like an actor playing a doctor. He wandered over to cute, mildly pear-shaped Nurse Bellamy.

"Nurse Bellamy, can I borrow a buck in quarters?" Dave batted his eyelashes, but the nurse shook her head.

"Why should I give you a loan, Dr. Richards?" she asked.

"Because if I don't have coffee, I can't save lives. Your quarters may be the difference between life and death."

"That's a new one." Nurse Bellamy dug in her purse and forked over the change. Dave grinned, headed over to the vending machine, and plunked the quarters in. He punched in the code for a cappuccino, but nothing came out.

"Come on." He shook the machine. He looked back at Nurse Bellamy who burst out laughing. Dave kicked the machine, then turned and saw a sullen Dr. Root walking toward him.

"Dr. Root, you got any spare change?"

Root looked up from Lacey's chart. "Where have you been?"

"Kind of crashed in room twenty-six. Just woke up."

Dr. Root was just about to deliver the bad news when he realized Dave—the star fellow from MIT, Dartmouth Medical School, and Harvard residency training—hadn't had his crack at Lacey. Dave smiled brightly and asked, "What's up?" Dr. Root handed him the file.

"I need you to pull a rabbit out of a hat."

Dave scanned the chart, instantly recognized the name, and headed for the room listed. Root followed, and as they walked, Dave rattled off a list of all the normal tests—and even the abnormal ones—that might be done in a situation like this.

"We've covered them all," Dr. Root assured him. "Dr. Richards, I have no idea what's happening to this patient. In fact, no one seems to." Dr. Root tried to temper his panic.

As they strode toward Lacey's room, Dave's eyes never left the chart.

"So, a normal healthy kid is suddenly paralyzed, and none of the finest minds can figure it out."

"Are you being sarcastic?"

"No. You've got a fine mind, Dr. Root. It doesn't control your urge to have extra helpings at dinner, but it's impressive nevertheless." Dr. Root wasn't in the mood for Dave's little digs.

Dave and Dr. Root arrived at Lacey's room in the ICU. Lacey looked pallid. Her heart was slowing as the machines in the ICU forced life into her. Dave quickly reviewed the chart and then looked over his shoulder to Dr. Root who stood in the doorway.

"Where's Dr. Paddock?"

"In my office," Dr. Root answered. But before he could inquire why Dave wanted to know, the young doctor brushed past him and rushed down the hall. Root ran behind him, but Dave was already sitting with the Paddocks when Root reached the waiting area. Root worried about how Dave would act with Dr. Paddock. He may have been brilliant, but he was hardly politically savvy. Still, Dave was that rare guy who could think outside the box.

"Dr. Paddock," Dave started. "Have you been on vacation recently?"

"What has that got to do with our daughter?" Kim snapped.

"Everything if you don't want to be sizing a casket."

Kim gasped and looked to her husband, who wasn't reacting. He just bit down on his lip and said, "We were in New York City. Saw some relatives." Dave shook his head, knowing that was a dead end.

"Where do you live?" Kim tried to interrupt again, and Dr. Paddock cut her off with a wave of his hand.

"Bel-Air, off Roscomare."

"Backyard. What's your backyard like?" Dave quickly asked.

"Very lush, lots of fruit trees."

Dave bolted out the door. Dr. Root and Dr. Paddock followed him and found Dave in the ICU with a confused nurse who was equally scared that Paddock's daughter was her patient. Dave stripped back Lacey's gown, checking every inch of her body. Root and Paddock stopped at the door of the ICU and watched Dave, who looked like a man possessed. Paddock hated to hope that this rude young doctor was finally onto something. He was afraid to hope that their nightmare was nearly over. Dr. Root started toward Dave, but Dr. Paddock held him back.

While Dave examined the girl, he could see his boss's reflection in a nearby mirror.

"We all love beautiful yards," Dave started. "They make us feel proud. In some ways, safer. But the truth is that the only way you're completely safe is to live in a post-asbestos apartment building." Dave turned Lacey over and searched through her mousy-brown hair. Dave continued narrating.

"That thing of beauty that you cherish usually has something waiting to kill you. Weird, huh? Sort of like a woman." The nurse blanched and stifled a retort. Dave froze; he felt something at the base of Lacey's skull.

"Tweezers," Dave demanded. The nurse was still fuming over the sexist shot.

"Hey, anytime today. Dying kid. Dad's kind of wondering what the hell you're doing."

The Nurse grabbed some tweezers and handed them to Dave. Dave pushed her hair out of the way and dug into the scalp in the back of Lacey's neck. There was a seeming tug of war. Dr. Paddock slowly moved forward, unsure what Dave was doing to his daughter. Dave cursed and pulled back the tweezers. Dave pulled back Lacey's hair to get a better view. Dave reached in with the tweezers and grabbed hold of something. Dave snapped at the nurse.

"There's gonna be some bleeding, so I suggest that you get, I dunno, a Band-Aid."

The nurse grabbed a kit out of a drawer. Dave's tug of war ended as he pulled an engorged tick out of the back of Lacey's neck.

"Got you, you little bastard." Dave gently crushed it between the tweezers and blanched at the parasite.

"It was just a nasty tick your kid picked up in the back yard. She should be fine." Dr. Paddock fell into a nearby chair, relief pouring through every inch of his body.

"A tick?" Dr. Root said, angry at himself for not thinking of something so obvious. Dave put the tick in a tray and handed it to the nurse.

"How could a tick do that to a baby?" the nurse asked.

"Ticks can carry bacteria like Lyme disease, but a California dog tick can inject a paralyzing toxin in its saliva as it feeds. In an adult you can just pick it out, but a baby can't." Dave told the nurse to get the tick over to etymology to find out more details. Kim Paddock arrived at the door, and Dave gave her the good news.

Lacey's recovery was rapid and remarkable as blood levels of the toxin slowly diminished. Dr. Paddock insisted that Dave personally oversee her case. There couldn't be any slipups, and clearly Dr. Dave Richards was not given to making errors.

While Dave worked on updating the chart, Dr. Root approached him.

"Well, I guess your future is secure," Dave said, smiling.

"I think it's the other way around."

"Don't think so. You're the one who hired me."

"But Paddock always considered you a 'get' for his department."

Dave didn't know how to respond. He wasn't aware he was thought of in that way. Dr. Root looked to Dave and said, "He pulled me aside and said that he was going to be forever grateful."

"Just like I said. Look, Paddock is known to be a man of his word."

"But you saved her life."

"But you were in charge. I'm just one of your tools. Being on his good side is going to take you a long way, buddy."

"Good thing I hired the wonder boy."

Dave looked at him and shook his head. He didn't consider himself a wonder boy, but he could see how Dr. Root could feel that way in light of the last several hours.

"It's time to knock off," Root started. "Why don't I buy you a drink at the Recovery Room?"

"Sure. I think some decompressing is in order."

The Recovery Room was an L-shaped bar between one of the Mann movie theaters and a Mexican restaurant. It was the nearest bar to the medical center and was started by a former nurse who got a large insurance settlement from a sex-discrimination lawsuit ten years back. She was no longer welcome in the hospital, so she started the Recovery Room. That way she could still see her friends after work.

Margaritas were two for one on Thursdays, and tequila was Dave's drink of choice. Patrón was the holy grail of tequila. It was pricey but did the job better than anything else on the shelf. Dave had discovered it one summer in Boston, when he decided not to go home after his third year at MIT. His mind was buzzing about what direction his career was going to take. It was that kind of buzzing and problem solving that made him an exceptional doctor, but it was also the kind of thing that kept him awake. A professor who had taken interest in his career had presented him with several career options: neurosurgery, toxicology, plastics, and ophthalmic surgery. These were all specialties he embraced, but the deeper question was how do you just suddenly decide your future for the next fifty years? His mind would wander through the options all night, and consequently he'd get no sleep. But the answer showed up in the form of an amber-colored bottle covered in Spanish. Patrón tequila. Not only did it go down easy, it would reduce his IQ from one hundred fifty to around ninety. And when your IQ is ninety, Dave realized, you sleep like a baby. Dave slept that whole summer in a roach-infested apartment on Mass Ave. When his buddies were up late at night on roach hunts shaking the critters out of an aging kitchen pegboard, he slept, courtesy of the Crossroads Bar around the corner and Señor Patrón. As his education went on, he would refer to Patrón, privately, as the cure. Now, ten years later, that hadn't changed.

Dr. Root and Dave scored a booth from an anxious couple who looked like they were on the first leg of a date.

Dave slid into the booth, and Dr. Root eased into his seat. The exhaustion of saving Lacey had just hit Root. He laid his head back and closed his eyes.

A tall blonde waitress approached. She had a hint of an accent Root couldn't identify. Dave suspected it was German, but she turned out to be Hungarian. "What can I get you?" the waitress asked sweetly.

"Sierra Nevada," Dr. Root said without opening his eyes. The waitress noticed that Dave was looking at the bar menu.

"I like the blue one," the waitress advised.

Dave looked up from the bar menu.

"The what?"

"The blue one. The blue margarita. It's the top seller."

"Sure, as long as there's two shots of Patrón, I'll go with the blue."

The waitress scribbled down the order on her pad and smiled. She headed to the bar, and Dave's eyes followed her.

Dr. Root opened his eyes, feeling slightly recharged.

"How did you do it?"

"Do what?"

"Figure out it was a tick?" Dr. Root asked.

"I went to medical school in New Hampshire. Did a lot of hiking and camping, and when I got back to the dorm one of them had dug into my ear. Since then, it's been an interest."

Dave sifted through some multicolored tortilla chips.

"If you hadn't been there that kid would have been dead by morning."

"It's no big deal. It's just how my mind works. I find things hiding in plain sight."

"Sometimes I feel like I'm in your shadow, and I'm your boss. But I'm okay with that, I guess. Are you?"

Dave rolled his eyes as the tall blonde waitress returned with their drinks.

"Ken, you like that chief-resident-boss crap. You like the paperwork and the politics. I just like, well…saving the day."

"So you'll settle for hero worship?"

"It's what I live for."

Dave sucked down half of his drink and thought about how well he was going to sleep that night.

Several minutes later a few of the other doctors doing their fellowship showed up at the Recovery Room. They all wanted to glad-hand the fair-haired boy of UCLA Medical. Maybe hanging around him would rub off. Maybe there was a secret they could bottle and use for their own careers. They all wanted to be near Dr. Richards to ensure they, too, would be on the cutting edge.

They were generous, each buying him a drink. His IQ dropped about fifteen points per shot, but he didn't feel he'd reached nirvana yet. The blue margaritas kept flowing.

Dave noticed that Dr. Root's phone kept making a dinging sound.

"Problem at the hospital?"

"No, the wife. Better get back."

"It's only nine," Dave said.

"She's anxious and pregnant. I gotta get going." Root grabbed his coat as Dave ordered another drink.

"Take it easy, Dr. Richards," Root warned playfully.

"I'm celebrating," Dave said.

"Have a good time."

Dave looked out the window and watched Dr. Root get into his car and drive off. The idea of being the wonder boy rolled around in his mind in a drunken haze. The more he drank the more he embraced the idea.

CHAPTER 5

2010

Dave Richards wasn't vain. He knew that women were attracted to him, so he seldom worried about his appearance. But that evening, in one of the CDC's less-traveled men's rooms, he looked in the mirror, and something caught his eye that he hadn't observed before. He cocked his head, puzzled, and then tapped the men's room light switch that turned on a light near the mirrors. As he edged closer, the fluorescent light gave his skin a ghoulish tinge. Dave realized he was developing crow's-feet. He wondered when that had happened. He turned forty-six a few months ago, and he was certain those tiny folds of skin hadn't been there then. Dave couldn't help but ponder whether his tequila-soaked binges over the last ten years had etched these grooves on his face. He fought back the notion that he had savaged his insides as well. His right hand reached around to press against his liver, but he quickly thought better of it. Dave couldn't bring himself to think what his weakness had wrought on his body. He had, without question, tested his liver's endurance with regularity. In med school his attention was piqued when the stoic yet wildly informative Professor Kern revealed the liver was the largest organ in the human body. Dave learned this vital organ had multiple functions: plasma protein synthesis, decomposition of blood cells, glycogen storage, and of course detoxification. Dave was filled with a deep unease when he thought about how he had treated his liver, the clutch player of the human body, to a never-ending assault of tequila-drenched days and nights. Though Dave had now been sober for three months, it didn't allay his fear that he may have done permanent damage. Dave sighed heavily and jumped as the bathroom door swung open with a high-pitched squeak and then slammed with a thud. Harley Cokliss, thick necked, came in and headed to a urinal. Harley was easily sixty pounds overweight and gasped for every breath of air as he padded across the cracked tile floor. His CDC badge bounced over his gut from side to side as he walked. When Harley saw Dave, there was a deep, awkward silence. Harley looked away and lined himself up at the stall. Dave was used to the cold shoulder. He was the source of regular gossip, due to his countless escapades of public drunkenness. There was a time he would have demanded respect from an IT guy like Harley, but not anymore. Dave mostly felt shame. Those waves of shame made him think about drinking again, but he thought of the twelve steps. He dropped his head a few inches and headed into the hall toward his office.

During his descent into infamy, Dave had been gradually moved from a corner office to offices further and further away from the CDC elite. Six months ago, he had come in to work and found his belongings stowed in a basement office. Dave never complained. He was grateful his stuff wasn't on the sidewalk.

Down in the basement, Dave surveyed his meager, stifling cubby of a room and brooded privately on how an MIT graduate could end up down here. Dave clearly knew the answer to his own question. It involved those daily declarations of admitting that he was an alcoholic. There was no one to blame but himself. Dave grabbed his car keys and headed up the dusty stairs.

As Dave reached the top, he spotted Dr. Root walking toward him. Dave's old friend Root was the last friendly face in the building. Root shook his hand, and they walked together silently down the corridor.

"How are you holding up?" Root asked.

"Been taking this new martial arts class. Kind of helps me stay centered."

"Well, good."

Dave looked up and saw his boss, Dr. Evan Lussier, the director of the CDC Counter-terrorism unit, rounding the corner. Lussier glanced toward Dave and Dr. Root. Lussier was a gaunt six foot four. Dave could tell he bought his suits off the rack to fit his extra-long arms so he didn't look like an ape. Dave didn't care for Lussier and believed he had attained the position because of political connections. Lussier didn't go to a prestigious medical school. And he wasn't at the top of the class. But he made the right donations to the right people. In terms of the new set of terrorism threats facing the country, Dave didn't consider Lussier the go-to guy. He just took the big title and made the go-to guys, such as Dr. Root, work for him.

Lussier looked away, clearly avoiding Dave. Dave noticed Lussier throw his arm around a petite Asian woman and duck into the nearest office. The door closed behind them.

"How's the classes…I mean sessions…going?" Root asked awkwardly. Dave looked back to Root.

"They call them AA meetings, and I've been going every day," Dave said.

They walked in uncomfortable silence past the door behind which the director had concealed himself. Dave looked over to Dr. Root.

"Any news on my review?"

"It hasn't been completed."

"It's just that I've gone to the mat here to make things right."

"Nate's birthday party is still burned into people's memories."

"I'm sorry about that."

"It's okay."

"No, it's not."

"Look, they say you've gotta hit bottom before you can get better. Nate's party was probably the best thing that could have happened to you," Root said.

"It took four waiters to break up the fight I started."

"But after that it was the only way I could get through to you. Get you to change your direction."

The morning after the party, Root sat Dave down and told him to get help or he'd be out the door. Dave finally got the message and, after several false starts, gave up the Patrón—the most difficult change he'd ever made in his life. He endured the withdrawals. His hands had a slight tremor, and he became deft at hiding it from his coworkers. But characteristic of Dave, he didn't give up, and eventually the amber bottle no longer ruled him.

Root looked into Dave's eyes when he spoke to him, something Dave appreciated.

"Look, I've always had your back," Root assured him. "I wouldn't be here if it wasn't for you. That fact has always been with me."

"Thanks."

"But Dr. Lussier is all about appearances. You know that. He thinks you're a pariah."

"Yeah, I guess I've always known that. Kind of stings to hear it out loud. Does that mean I'm done for here?"

"No. Not yet. But I'm not going to lie to you. It's touch and go," Dr. Root said plainly. "Your position is performance based, and he's stuck you in the basement doing paperwork on cases no one actually cares about."

"The job's all I've got," Dave forced out, looking down at his feet, embarrassed.

"You know I'll always do what I can to help you, Dave."

"Well, you always have."

Dave shook Dr. Root's hand. Root noted that Dave's once-firm handshake was decidedly weaker. Dave's eyes revealed a talented man who'd been beaten up by the bottle. He could scarcely believe that Dr. Dave Richards's life had come to this. Root patted Dave on the back, and Dave headed out the lobby doors.

Dave hopped into his powder blue Toyota Celica and headed out onto Clifton Road. Soon he was on the James Wendell George Parkway driving through Atlanta. He had caught a lucky break with the traffic. It usually didn't bunch up until six, but it was almost six now and still clear sailing.

He spied Piedmont Park, and it brought a rare smile. He had proposed to his wife Meredith near one of the fountains seven years ago. Dr. Root's wife Emily had introduced them. Emily and Meredith worked for Balin Pharmaceutical. The drug companies employed very attractive women to push their wide array of medicines. Emily and Meredith fit the bill.

Dave was immediately charmed by Meredith's elegant Southern charm. Over the years he had become wiser when it came to women. He'd found that most important trait in a woman was kindness. It was a lesson he learned after being attracted to too many high-maintenance women. He thought they were exciting and engaging but soon tired of the all-consuming chaos.

Meredith was five foot nine and shapely with long dark brown hair and hazel eyes. She looked Italian, but her background was Dutch-Irish. Dave's mother liked Meredith. She called her "Scarlett O'Hara with a soul."

The Toyota sputtered as Dave got off the exit. He turned down a tree-lined street and pulled up to tan-colored traditional home in a development that bordered Druid Hills. Dave stopped the car and parked. Meredith was in the front yard, wearing her gardening gloves with her hair tied back. She was pruning the rose bushes that lined the right side of the house.

Meredith turned around and saw Dave. Her pleasant smile grew cold as Dave approached.

"Hi," Dave said quietly.

"What are you doing here?"

"I got off early. Figured I'd check up on you. Got a martial arts class nearby. Wing Chun. Interesting stuff. You learn how to move in darkness and fight with your eyes closed. "

Meredith went back to pruning bushes, disinterested. "Well, I am fine. So you can get on to your class."

"I've been sober for three months," Dave blurted out. "Thought you'd like to know."

Meredith looked into his eyes, then down. "That's great, Dave. I'm happy for you." She turned and walked back toward the bushes.

"But you won't take me back."

"I'm not ready. And twelve weeks is great Dave, but it's only twelve weeks. I can't trust twelve weeks."

"I've changed, though. I want you to know that."

"Now, I need to get this done. I'm going out to dinner tonight."

Dave didn't ask with whom. He didn't dare. He wanted desperately to get back with Meredith, so he knew asking about her private life would be a bad move.

"Sorry I bothered you. I just wanted to see you."

Dave got into his Toyota. The engine gasped and sputtered and then started on the second try. Meredith watched Dave drive off and disappear behind a thick hedge three houses down. Meredith stood there and started to cry. She wiped her tears on her sleeve and looked around to see if the neighbors had noticed.

Meredith went back to tending her yard and Dave went back to his tiny studio apartment, five miles away, to change for his Wing Chun class.

CHAPTER 6

PRESENT DAY

Ben Curran hadn't grown more than three inches in the last thirteen years. He was five nine and three quarters and had given up hope he'd reach five ten. Ben looked down the airstrip; its tar was cracked, and weeds had sprouted trying to consume the runway. It was a desolate, silent place with the exception of the windsock that snapped and fluttered with a breeze from the southeast.

Ben looked at his watch and wondered where the others were. A sound drew his attention. He could see a trail of dust kicking up in the distance. Someone was coming down the dirt road that led to what had been Carleton Airport. It wasn't much of an airport anymore. The one hangar had been burned down on Halloween four years back, but it had been vacant since the airport had gone into receivership in the eighties.

The GMC Yukon that was kicking up the trail of dust raced up to Ben and came to a halt.

Rance Gutchens, a sixty-year-old, scraggly bearded man, hopped out of the truck. He headed straight for Ben and pumped his hand. Two others jumped out and joined them: Zack Heaton, a thirty-five-year-old with a crew cut sporting a Ted Nugent T-shirt that crept up over his belly, and Johnny Dodge. Johnny was Ben's age, and they had gone to Groton High together. Johnny was lean, bespectacled, and had a unibrow. Kids used to call him "Cro-Magnon." Ben had always stood up for him. Johnny was always there for Ben. When Ben suggested they join the Knights of the White Order, Johnny signed up with him.

Rance looked up at the gray sky and then looked at his watch. He shook it to make sure it was working.

"He's late," Rance said with a tinge of scorn. Ben pointed to the windsock. It had been flapping in the same direction all morning.

"Headwinds from the southeast. It's probably slowing them down. Gotta be twenty-mile-an-hour winds." Rance turned toward the windsock and nodded. Rance looked back to Johnny, who was playing footsie with an errant weed on the tarmac.

"Johnny, get the money out of the car."

Johnny strode over to the Yukon, pulled out a knapsack, and walked it back over to Rance. Rance peeked inside the knapsack and counted the bundles of money. Ben looked into the bag over Rance's shoulder, curious. Rance closed the knapsack, giving him a dirty look. Ben backed off, and they waited in silence for several minutes. Ben kept shifting his stance, and Rance asked him what was wrong.

"Gotta take a leak," Ben said. Rance told him to be quick about it, and Ben double-timed it toward the woods that bordered the airfield. Ben didn't like peeing in front of other people. He'd been that way since he was kid. He found a thick tree, hid behind it, and unzipped.

As the wind slightly rocked him in the breeze, Ben's mind drifted back to the days after his parents were killed. Ben's childhood and his innocence were crushed after the carnage in Idaho. He didn't have any relatives, so he was put into the foster care system until he reached eighteen. The foster parents who took him in were indifferent to Ben and clearly were only interested in the monthly check from the state.

He was exceptional in school and got high marks, but that didn't spur the foster parents to care any more. He continued to read voraciously. Ben became a fan of spy thrillers. He read John Le Carre, Robert Ludlum, and Ian Fleming from cover to cover. He liked reading about men who made their own rules. He wanted to be like them. It created a passion for justice within him.

Ben, on advice from an old friend of his father's, engaged the services of a local lawyer, Henry Heath. Ben wanted justice, and Henry assured the brokenhearted sixteen-year-old that he would get him a large paycheck out of the feds for killing his mom. But Ben didn't realize that Henry Heath was no match for the power and legal might of the Department of Justice. Henry Heath, who graduated from Loyola Marymount Law School, was going up against names like Jud Kenley, who made the Harvard Law Review when he was only twenty. Kenley's second chair was Oscar Deschamps, Yale Law and the first in his class. Ben would learn the hard way that he didn't have even a remote chance of getting justice. Ben saw his lawyer being out-classed and out-spent. The case wound its way through the court system for four years. The only benefit that came out of it was that they were treated to a free education from two lawyers from Harvard and Yale. Henry Heath retreated to a life settling insurance claims, and Ben retreated to despair. He would not even be compensated for his parents' deaths; no one would ever pay. It didn't make sense to Ben, as the heroes in the books he loved always got justice. He couldn't understand where he went wrong. He resolved to reread the novels he'd read and wouldn't rest until he found the answer. He didn't sleep for two days while he went on a marathon reading session. His foster parents did finally notice that their charge was starting to suffer from exhaustion. It wasn't until he was on his third day without sleep that they acted and had him hospitalized.

His stay in the hospital psych ward was short, but while he was there he started to reach some clarity. He had to distrust the legal system because it was rigged. His father was right. It was part of everything Harlan Curran despised.

After his brief stay in the hospital, Ben joined the Knights of the White Order. He was going to get his revenge for the murder of his parents. He was going to show the government of the United States of America that they couldn't crush him. He hoped someday his actions would make them pay dearly for the pain they had inflicted on him. Ben was committed to follow in his father's footsteps, and that's how he found himself standing in the middle of a deserted, windswept airfield.

Ben heard the late-model Piper Cherokee approaching. He tried to hurry up, but it came out of the clouds in an instant. The cloud ceiling was low, so the plane hit the tarmac within a minute of appearing. It taxied over to Rance and his men, blowing Zack's hat off as it passed. Ben peeked around the tree and could see Rance glancing back toward the trees, probably looking for Ben.

The plane came to a stop, and the door popped open. Ben could see Fred Sommers hopping down from the wing of the plane. Ben had met Fred once, and he felt he was best described with one word: greasy. His hair was greasy, his skin was oily, and so was his personality. His teeth were a rare shade of yellow, and he had a distinct body odor he would never forget.

Ben zipped up and started out toward the plane. He could see Rance handing Fred a knapsack. Fred opened it and counted the money. Rance looked over to Ben and urged him to hurry up.

Zack popped open the smallish cargo hatch and pulled out an array of machine guns, grenades, heavy machine guns, sniper rifles, and a treasure trove of other weaponry.

Ben picked up his pace as he saw Johnny and Zack loading the Yukon with the guns, while Fred and Rance completed their deal with a handshake.

Ben was halfway across the field when five black ATF cars came zooming out of the woods on the other side of the airfield. Ben froze and then reached for the thirty-eight-caliber snub nose in his waistband.

Fred Sommers hopped into his Cherokee and got the engine started. He didn't even close the door or put on his seat belt before he started the plane.

When they heard the warning shots fired from the agents who were rapidly closing in, Rance, Zack, and Johnny ran for the Yukon. Rance looked toward Ben. Ben pulled out his gun, and Rance tried to wave him off. Ben began backing toward the woods.

He saw the Piper Cherokee racing down the field at a good clip, about to go into its takeoff roll. The engine revved up, and the wheels left the ground.

One of the agents ran to the center of the runway, pointed his M-16 at the Piper Cherokee, and squeezed the trigger, burping out bullets. The slugs ripped into the thin aluminum plane, igniting the wing tanks. The plane dipped and smacked into the end of the runway at a thirty-degree angle, then exploded into a fireball.

Ben recoiled at the sight of Fred Sommers crashing through the windshield. His body rolled about an eighth of a mile, eventually putting out the fire that had almost consumed him. Now Fred Sommers's body smoked in the southeastern breeze, singed bills fluttering around his corpse.

The plane's reserve tank blew up as the agents handcuffed Rance, Zack, and Johnny. Ben could see Rance, who was on the ground and looking toward him. Rance shook his head indicating Ben should run. Ben started backing toward the woods when he heard an agent call out.

"We got another one!" Ben could hear radios crackling and then saw several agents setting out after him.

"Halt. ATF!" Moltidani screamed while pulling out his Glock from his holster.

"Halt," he yelled one more time.

Ben sprinted away. He didn't know these woods well, so he prayed he wasn't running into a dead end. He poured on the steam, ducking branches and trees. He heard the agents behind him. Ben was lost. He wasn't sure which way to go. He stopped behind a tree, pulled out his gun, and fired off two shots. He hoped that would slow them down while he figured out which way to go.

Ben heard a bullet sail past his head and saw it explode in a tree three yards ahead of him. Ben turned right and fought through a thicket of brush. He fired back two more shots at the agents. He only had two more bullets left. He wasn't sure what he was going to do. He couldn't believe everything had gone so badly. The sight of Fred Sommers's burning body flying out of the Piper Cherokee would haunt him, joining the deaths of his parents in the bilge of his mind.

Five more shots rang out, but they were way off target. Ben fired back one round and heard a distant scream. He must have hit one of the agents.

Moltidani charged ahead, emptying a fresh fifteen-round clip in Ben's direction.

Ben fired off his last shot just as he heard the sound of a car zooming by just beyond the trees. Ben squeezed through a thicket and found himself standing on a one-lane highway with a semi bearing down on him. The semi's driver hit the brakes and came to a squealing stop not a foot away from Ben.

Ben heard the driver's door open. He peered down at his spent pistol and then eyed the pair of feet hitting the pavement on the other side of the truck. Ben needed a friend; but Ben wouldn't look too friendly with a snub nose in his hand, so he tossed the gun underneath the truck. Ed Guyler came around to where Ben was standing. The guy looked about fifty and had a kind face underneath his Cat Diesel cap.

"You okay, son?"

"Yeah." Ben looked back toward the woods.

"You need a lift? I'm headed to Boise."

"That'd be fine. Yeah, sure." Ben hopped in the truck but kept an eye on the woods. Ed settled into his seat and adjusted the radio. He asked Ben if the station was okay. It was all country all the time, and he understood not everyone went for the twangy music.

"Sure, not a problem."

"Mind if I smoke?" Ed asked.

"No, its fine with me."

Ed looked through the glove compartment for some matches. Ben tried not to look anxious as Ed fumbled through the cluttered truck. Ben looked in the rearview mirror and still saw no sign of the agents. Ed found some matches and lit up a cigarette.

Ed threw the semi into gear, and the truck rumbled off down the road.

An hour later, Ed dropped Ben off in Boise, gave him a friendly handshake, and wished him well.

Ben stood outside of a McDonald's, unsure of what he should do. He considered going home to Salmon River and then realized his gun had his fingerprints on it and soon they'd identify him. Besides, it was likely that one of his compatriots would finger him. Rance, Johnny, and Zack had become his makeshift family. Now that was torn apart. Ben was alone again. He had to get away before he was grabbed and thrown in jail. He couldn't go to jail. He had a mission to complete. God had put him on this path for a reason, and he had to answer the call.

Ben went around a corner and saw his bank, Hanover Savings and Loan. Ben calmly strode in and closed his account. He had eight thousand dollars: three thousand left from his mother's insurance policy, and five thousand from a Wal-Mart robbery Rance and the others had pulled off three months ago. Ben got a cab downtown to the bus station. They'd be watching the airports, and he'd get out of town quicker on a bus.

Ben stepped into the bus station. It was worn down. The floors, originally white linoleum, were gray with age. There were scattered benches that had also seen better days.

Ben scanned the board of destinations. A cop car pulled up outside, and Ben turned his back, fearfully. He moved up to the ticket agent.

"Which bus is leaving next?"

"Bus for New York leaves in five minutes."

Ben quickly plunked down cash. The puzzled ticket agent gave him a long look. Ben noticed the distrust in his eyes.

"I thought I missed it," Ben said. "My watch has been on the fritz. If I missed that bus my grandmother would have killed me." The ticket agent smiled.

"We'll get you there in time. Randy's driving, and he has the best on-time performance of any driver in the Greyhound family," the ticket agent said.

"Where are your bags?" the ticket agent asked.

"I left them outside."

"Son, you're going to New York City. You never leave your bags unattended. Hope your grandmother's meeting you at the station."

"She sure is."

The ticket agent smiled and handed Ben his ticket.

"Thanks for the advice."

Ben took his seat and looked out the window. He could see the cop milling about the station. Ben gripped the armrests. He spotted a bus driver headed for this bus, but he passed by. Ben prayed the driver would hurry up. Then he heard a thunk, followed by another thunk. The baggage doors were being closed.

Randy, the driver with the best on-time performance in the Greyhound family, stepped up into his driver's seat, grabbed the microphone, and announced to the passengers their destination was New York City. The doors closed with a hydraulic hiss. He turned the engine on, and the bus shook with a low rumble. He put the bus in gear, and they moved out of the station.

Ben leaned back in his chair, his hands unclenching. He closed his eyes, but all he could see was Fred Sommers's smoking carcass. He pressed his head against the window, watching the great expanse of Idaho passing him. He wondered if he'd ever come home again. Idaho, the only place in the world he knew, could be slipping into his past forever.

CHAPTER 7

Randy, the pride and joy of Greyhound, drove the leviathan of a bus into Port Authority at three a.m. He deftly parked his bus in the assigned slot for arrivals from Idaho. He fingered the loudspeaker button.

"Welcome to New York City, New York," he proudly announced. "Please wait outside the vehicle for your stowed luggage."

The passengers were already rising from their seats, stretching their legs, and moving toward the front of the bus. Randy hit the door release, which opened with a soft hiss. Randy bounded out the door and opened the duel baggage bays.

Ben Curran was the first off the bus. He had slept for the last ten hours. He woke up as they came through the eastern end of Pennsylvania. Ben was absorbed by the awesome size of New York with a childlike sense of wonder. Ben had seen pictures of

New York City his whole life, but nothing could have prepared him for its majesty. He had assumed it would be like downtown Boise, but nothing could have been further from the truth. People don't whisper in New York, he observed—they screech. Their voices were as tall as the buildings.

The energy of the city was palpable. It both intrigued and frightened him. The people weren't like the people in Idaho. They were black and Asian and Hispanic and, in some cases, unidentifiable. A cacophony of languages surrounded him. There was a couple speaking in French, he suspected, and then two men speaking in Chinese in front of a hot dog stand. Maybe coming to New York was a mistake. The enemy was everywhere. He could see the people that were encroaching on what white America had built. Ben wished he could wash them all away and clean the city of these vermin, but the time wasn't right. Ben had to wait for the right opportunity.

Ben walked up to an information booth and zipped up his thin jacket. All he had were the clothes on his back and the eight thousand dollars in his pocket. A stern, thick, black woman in a tight-fitting Port Authority uniform looked up at Ben.

"Can I help you?"

"I need to find a hotel. I just got into town."

"What's your price range?"

"Pardon?"

"Hotel, motel? Price range?"

"Clean and not dangerous."

"The Embassy Suites is five blocks uptown. Cab stands outside. Welcome to New York."

She gave him a bright smile. Ben forced a smile back and headed out of Port Authority into the windy night.

He pulled his jacket around him. Standing in its midst the city seemed even more overwhelming. He saw a row of cabs lined up. Ben approached the first cab in line. The cab driver looked up at Ben.

"Where are you headed?"

"The Embassy Suites."

"I know it. Get in."

The cab driver drove Ben to the hotel. A drenching rain began pounding the roof of the yellow cab. Ben couldn't see where he was going. The driver could be driving in circles, and he'd never know.

The cab came to stop in front of the Embassy Suites. There were several cars ahead of them, so they couldn't park under the awning. Ben tipped the cab driver well and ran through the sheets of rain toward the lobby.

He checked in and tried to get some more sleep, but that wasn't in the cards. He had to make plans. Ben had to figure out his next step. He sat in his room and watched TV until he heard a thump at the door. Ben got up and opened it and saw a *New York Post* sitting on the hallway rug. He looked down to the end of the hall and saw a sprightly Latino kid tossing papers at each door. He disappeared around the corner, but Ben could still hear the newspapers slamming down, getting fainter and fainter.

Ben retreated to his room with the paper and found a coffee maker. He made a pot and sat and read the paper. He sat at the table and tried to concentrate on the latest developments with the European Union, but his mind was racing. He spied a cardboard stand on a pseudo-mahogany table. He picked it up and was reminded that the Embassy Suites offered a free breakfast starting at six.

Ben gathered up his paper and headed down into the breakfast room. He was the first one to arrive. The smell of bacon and eggs brought back memories of his mom. Ben smiled and went over to the breakfast line. Everything was fresh, and he had two helpings of everything.

Ben continued to scan the paper and stopped cold when he spotted the story about the Knights of The White Order. There was a picture of Rance surrounded by several ATF agents. Rance was in shackles and looked weary. It was clear from the picture he knew what was in store for him. He'd die in prison, and nothing was going to change that.

Ben rifled through the pages to see if he was mentioned. He read it over and over and then realized he had missed the last section on a third page. He tore through the paper frantically and found the last two paragraphs stuck between a meth lab explosion story and a crooked cop piece.

Ben was conscious of his own breathing as he read. The story mentioned that they were hunting for the fifth person, Ben Curran. They detailed his activities and mentioned that they had solid leads on his whereabouts. Had the ticket taker remembered him and said he'd headed to New York?

Ben headed to a newsstand in the motel and bought a few more papers. He found the same story in the *New York Times* and then found his picture in the *Philadelphia Inquirer*. Ben wondered who had flipped on him. Johnny wouldn't have; he looked up to him like an older brother. Zack was the good soldier type; the ATF could never break him. It had to be Rance. If he didn't flip on Ben he'd spend the rest of his life in prison, but this didn't keep Ben from being blind with anger. Rance had become a surrogate father to Ben. Harlan Curran would never have caved like that.

Ben could see a man in the corner reading the *Inquirer* and turned away. He knew he had to think quickly. The first place the ATF would look would be the motels. He had checked in under an assumed name, but they had his picture and would show it to every hotel clerk in the city. He needed to disappear. He needed to find an apartment. Fortunately, there was an ad section in the paper offering different rentals around the city.

He rifled through the pages and had instant sticker shock. There were a few studio apartments that featured a hot plate instead of a kitchen. Those were going for twelve hundred a month. It meant he'd only have enough cash for four or five months, but he'd have to figure out his cash flow situation later. If he were in an apartment, he'd be safe. He'd be off the radar. New York was an easy place to get lost in, and he needed to take advantage of it.

He bought a pay-as-you-go cell phone from a T-Mobile kiosk and called several of the ads. The first to answer was a gruff apartment manager.

"The last guy who lived in the room killed himself. So I don't want any crap about it. Not giving any goddamn price breaks `cause some guy cacked himself in my building," the manager said.

"Sure, okay. When could I see it?

"Come right over."

Ben checked out of the Embassy Suites and found a nearby subway entrance. He examined the maps on the dingy walls and asked a few locals how to use the subway system. He wasn't prepared for the screeching metal on metal of the subway. He didn't know what was more confusing: the directions on the wall of the subway or the helpful New Yorkers who talked too fast to understand.

Ben got lost a few times but eventually came up the subway steps that dropped him off on the Lower East Side. The building was a mere block from the stop. A lucky break.

Ben hit the buzzer, and the manager, who never offered his name, showed him the studio apartment. It was clean and neat. The furniture from the previous occupant was still there. According to the manager, he had been a dancer who had come to try to make it on Broadway and clearly didn't. The gruff manager said he could have all the stuff taken out by the end of the day.

"You can leave it," Ben said.

The manager asked for two months' rent up front, and Ben paid him in cash. Ben took the keys and asked, "How'd he do it?" The manager looked around to him.

"How'd who do what?"

"How'd he kill himself?"

"He jumped." The manager closed the door after him. Ben walked to the window and looked down into the alley. It was eight floors down. The police tape was still there. Ben closed the window and surveyed the room. There were books on theater, the arts, and gay lifestyles. Though Ben's tolerance for other races was low, he held homosexuality in even lower regard. It was a sin against God, and he knew he had to wash the sins out of his new home.

The basement of the building had cold gray walls and numerous water stains etched into the concrete. It featured three washers and three dryers, all coin operated. Ben loaded the linens from the room and set the heat level on high. He needed to burn the perversions out of those sheets. Ben was waiting for the laundry on a rickety chair when the door swung open and two Arab men in sandals and sweats entered, carrying a basket heaped with clothes. They were chattering away in Arabic. They were having a serious discussion and stopped when they saw Ben. Then they turned around and left the laundry room.

Ben thought that curious. There were plenty of washers, but they didn't want to do their laundry in front of him. It didn't make any sense. They were the invaders; he should be shunning them, not the other way around.

Ben later found out the Arabs lived on his floor, three doors down. They lived four to a room in a one-bedroom apartment. One was clearly older than the rest. He was in his fifties, while the others were in their twenties.

The days were long and listless for Ben. He had no one to talk to. He reasoned he just had to lay low and hope the ATF didn't pick up his trail. But he needed something to do. He traveled outside sparingly so he wouldn't be spotted. Ben assumed his picture had been plastered all over, and it would be better if he didn't make it easy for them.

He did make a trip to the local drugstore to buy some hair dye. He dyed his hair black and noted that his appearance changed radically. It took a week or so to get used to looking at himself in the mirror. But as he felt a little more invisible, he ventured out more. He took long walks in the city. New York never seemed to end, and he had all the time in the world to take it in.

Three weeks after he moved in, he noticed one of his Arab neighbors taking pictures of a power station. Ben thought it odd that anyone would take a picture of a component of the city's electric grid. The Arab slung the camera around his neck, jammed his hands in his pockets, and headed uptown against a cold, whipping wind. Ben followed the Arab and was careful to stay a block or so behind him. The Arab walked at a brisk clip and expertly navigated the sea of pedestrians. Ben had a hard time keeping up. When the Arab turned a corner, Ben lost him. Ben broke into a run, turning the same corner, but the Arab was gone. There was no way that the guy could have disappeared that quickly. Ben spun around, figuring he must have missed something. He had. There was a cyber café at the corner. Ben looked in the window and saw the Arab paying for a card.

Ben entered the cyber café. It was ultra modern, featuring chairs with more style than function. The place was packed with Dell computers. The café was L-shaped, and Ben had to peek around a corner to see the Arab. He was sitting at the computer that was the furthest from the rest of the customers. Ben sat at a nearby computer and spied on the Arab.

The Arab set his digital camera on the computer table. He pulled out a long cord and plugged it into the CPU. He got online in an instant, uploaded the pictures, and e-mailed them to parts unknown. The Arab opened the camera and took the card out and closed it. He got up and strode past Ben. Ben rose and followed him.

The man fingered the camera card between thumb and forefinger. Ben stayed close as the man continued uptown. When the man reached a bus stop, he looked around, flicked the camera card down to the ground, and kicked it into a sewer drain. Ben stopped. The Arab boarded a bus and rode out of sight.

While Ben walked toward his apartment, he tried to digest what he had just seen. Why would the Arab toss a camera card away like it was garbage? But, more importantly, why would he throw it into a drain? Ben quickly surmised that the Arab was hiding something and decided that he was going to make the Arabs in 8C his project.

The following week, Ben kept his eye on the Arabs. They usually didn't go out together, so he kept switching which one he'd tail. It was obvious that they were up to something. They didn't have jobs—or did they? Ben got it in his head that he had stumbled upon a terrorist cell. They regularly bought pay-as-you-go phones and tossed them. They seemed to be obsessed with taking pictures and video. Ben was intrigued. Ben began formulating an idea, an idea that would finally put him on his true path.

Assir Katafi was in the laundry room loading the whites into a plastic laundry basket. Ben entered and stood in the doorway. Assir looked up at Ben, stoically finished loading his laundry, and started to leave but found Ben in his way.

"Excuse me," Assir said politely. Ben didn't move. He just looked Assir over.

"What's your name?" Ben asked.

"Assir. I am in a hurry."

"To take some more pictures?" Ben asked.

Assir looked at him, his eyes widening. Ben assumed that Assir thought he was a federal agent and had somehow found him out.

"I don't know what you mean."

"You and your friends seem to like to take a lot of pictures." Assir put the basket down on a washer. Ben heard some footsteps coming down the stairs, and Khalid, a tall fierce-looking Arab, appeared behind Ben. Ben looked around and realized he was the same one he first tailed a week ago.

"I know what you guys are doing," Ben said. Assir shot Khalid a look of concern and looked back to Ben.

"I don't understand," Khalid said, smiling.

"You're a sleeper cell. You're here to try to kill Americans." Khalid went silent. He moved toward Ben and closed the laundry room door behind him.

"Why do you say such things?"

Ben smiled and sat on the edge of a flimsy card table. He reveled in making these two subhumans nervous. Ben crossed his arms and looked at one, then the other.

"I've been following you for the last week—Brooklyn Bridge, power stations, Empire State Building—and I don't think you're tourists."

Khalid started toward Ben and Ben rose. Assir froze in the corner, not sure what their next move should be.

"I'm not your enemy," Ben said forcefully. "We want the same thing." Khalid backed off. He wasn't sure where this was going.

"Who are you?" Khalid demanded.

"A friend."

"He's FBI," Assir snapped. "Let's get out of here."

"I'm not FBI. I'm just a like-minded citizen looking for the right opportunity."

Khalid looked at this dark-haired American with deep confusion. Assir edged toward the door, and Khalid stuck out his hand, holding him back.

"You said you're like minded," Khalid started. "How are you like minded?"

"Well, we both hate the government of the United States, and we both feel the way to make them listen is to kill Americans."

"Look, you guys stand out like sore thumbs. You've got three hundred million eyes on you. Anywhere you go, Americans assume you're terrorists, but no one expects an all-American boy like me. I can help you. Of course there'd be money involved."

Ben noticed Khalid's body relax.

CHAPTER 8

Oren Zakah prayed to Mecca three times a day. He was supposed to pray five times, performing the salah. He recited the prayer prostrate, performing his final raka'ah, and then recited the complete Tashahhud, as he had done most of his life.

Oren was fifty and slightly paunchy. He was a Saudi by birth and had become an engineer until anger, fed by Osama Bin Laden, set him on a different path. He looked at Assir, who was sipping some tea on the couch. Khalid came out of the bathroom and sat next to Assir. Khalid looked to Oren for some direction. They had been speaking about the conversation they'd had with Ben Curran and were trying to figure out what the next step would be. Oren was the leader of the cell, and they counted on his direction.

"You believe him?" Oren asked. Khalid nodded quickly. "If he was FBI, we'd have already been arrested."

"True. They'd observe us until we were further along."

"I think we should listen to him."

"Still, there's danger," Oren warned.

"We're not in contact with any other cells," Khalid said. "There's no danger of him making contact with other groups."

"But how do we know if he can be trusted?"

"A loyalty test."

Oren's cell replaced two men that had been sent to New York three years ago, and they had lost contact. They never carried out their mission, and they didn't respond to any of the dead-drop messages sent to them.

Oren's job was to start a new cell and find out what happened to Raffi Adalah and Ayin Tabul. Oren left his fellow cell members, Assir, Khalid, and Tunis, to the business of preparation for an attack. Oren's job was to find Raffi and Ayin. He had picked up their trail a few weeks ago and had discovered that they were no longer believers in the cause. They had American girlfriends and American jobs. They were living the good Western life in Greenwich Village. The years of training in terrorist camps had been erased by an easy American life.

Oren discovered that they were consumed by everything that he hated. They had even changed their names to Chuck and Rick. They were working for Verizon and making solid commissions.

Oren had written up a report and placed it in the dead drop near the U.N. The next dead-drop pickup contained orders from the Gulf. Raffi and Ayin were to be terminated. They had to pay for their betrayal. Oren hadn't signed up to be an assassin. In his mind there was a difference between killing someone face-to-face and organizing a large terrorist operation. He didn't want any of his men to do it because things could go wrong. Evidence could somehow lead back to them, and he couldn't allow that.

Oren looked to Khalid and told him how Ben Curran could prove his loyalty. Khalid leaned forward and listened intently as Oren gave him his orders.

The humidity was oppressive as he walked through Greenwich Village. He went down Bleecker and turned onto MacDougal. His heart was pounding hard. Ben had never killed anyone before, and he was about to kill two men. They were subhuman in his book but, nevertheless, the word human was in there somewhere. He checked the bowie knife that was tucked into his jacket. It was sharp, and he nearly pricked his finger as he searched for it. He stopped at the foot of a brownstone. He pulled out a slip of paper with the targets' address and jammed it back into his pocket.

A sexy, freckled redhead came bounding out the front door, and Ben caught it before it closed. Ben found a small elevator and got in. It was rickety and loud and said it could carry up to four hundred pounds. He doubted that. His one-hundred-and-sixty-five-pound frame made the elevator struggle, but finally it stopped on the fifth floor.

Ben stepped out and pulled out two pictures of Raffi and Ayin. He studied them. There couldn't be any mistakes. Oren had given him this job as an act of faith. If he completed it, he'd gain the Arabs' trust and access to their considerable resources. Ben was going to do his father's bidding and get revenge for his mother's death. He just had to pull this off.

Ben found room 505. As he approached it, the door opened and out stepped a short, curly-haired blonde carrying a knapsack. She was obviously a college student. She turned and kissed the man at the door—Raffi. She brushed past Ben and got into the elevator.

Ben swallowed hard. He hadn't counted on anyone else being there. He didn't want to have to kill the girlfriend. That would be sloppy. He felt relieved when the elevator door closed and she headed down with it. He needed to terminate his two targets and escape. This was the right moment. The elevator would take at least two minutes to go down, which meant no one could make his way up until another two. That left him four minutes to do what he came for.

Ben could hear his heart slamming inside of his chest. He couldn't understand why he was so nervous. He was finally taking action. He was removing a pair of invaders. His father would be proud. He kept repeating to himself in his head: "If you ain't white, you ain't right." His heart didn't slow down no matter how many times he recited his mantra. Ben was angry with himself. He shouldn't be nervous—he should be exhilarated.

Ben reached 505 and was about to knock on the door, when he realized that the curly-haired blonde hadn't properly closed the door.

Ben brought his foot up to the door and carefully and ever so slowly swung the door open. He could hear the shower running in one of the bedrooms. Some Arabic music was playing. One of the men had to be in the shower. That was a lucky break. He couldn't kill two men at a time. When Ben reached the kitchen, Raffi was at the counter with his back to the door. He was opening a container of muffins. Ben pulled out his bowie knife and crept toward him.

Raffi scooped up a blueberry muffin, took an inhumanly large bite, and washed it down with some tea that was sitting on the counter. Ben could smell the mint tea as he stepped closer. Ben closed the distance between him and Raffi. Ben's hand was quivering, and he cursed his own weakness. He had to do this for his father and his mother. This was his time to shine.

The time between the moment Ben was holding the knife and the moment he plunged it into Raffi's neck was a blank. Blood sprayed like water from a gardening hose. Raffi wailed and held up his hands in mercy. Ben cut him across the throat and then made a downward jab into his chest. Raffi spun around and stumbled backward, hitting his head on the sink. Raffi's life drained out of him quicker than Ben imagined it would. Ben looked around and saw Ayin at the door to his bedroom, naked and carrying a towel.

When Ayin realized what was happening, he rolled out the open window onto the fire escape. Ben launched himself forward. He raced after Ayin, who ran, in a panic.

Ayin hadn't gone far when he stepped on a broken beer bottle and screamed. Ben was on top of him in short order, plunging his bowie knife into the man over and over. Ben let out all his anger on Ayin. He kept stabbing him even after he was clearly dead.

When Ben stood up, he realized his heart was no longer racing; he was calm. He felt completely at peace. He stepped over Ayin's bloody corpse and made his way down the fire escape.

He calmly walked around a dumpster that was in the alley. He found the bag he had placed there the night before. Ben stripped off his bloody clothes. He grabbed a towel and wiped himself clean. He pulled out a jumpsuit and donned it with speed and precision. He stuffed his bloody clothes and the towel back in the bag, walked out of the alley, and headed back down MacDougal.

Two blocks down, Ben passed a late-model Nissan. Oren was behind the wheel, and the back driver's-side window was down. Ben tossed the bag in the backseat and continued walking like nothing had happened.

Oren opened the bag, reached in. He pulled his hand out and looked at the blood on his hand.

Ben heard a scream in the distance and assumed it had come from the apartment building. He looked back and saw Oren getting out of the car. Ben walked with a little spring in his step as he heard more screams and shouting. Ben was hungry. He had decided not to eat before his job in case he was tempted to vomit. He didn't want to leave DNA evidence at the scene. But now he was famished. He passed an IHOP and stepped inside.

The killings had been easier than Ben could have imagined. In fact, he felt more grief when he shot a squirrel when he was ten. The only feeling Ben had after taking out the two targets was a great sense of release.

CHAPTER 9

Dr. Hiram Dunn had a look of concern. He had to talk to the Munsen family about their son who had collapsed on a softball field in Hope, Arkansas, earlier that day. He had to give them an update on his condition.

Dr. Dunn was fifty and sported a goatee. His wore round horn-rimmed glasses that gave him an almost comical look.

He pushed the door and entered the waiting room. Al and Zoe Munsen looked up. Al shook his hand, and Dunn filled them in.

"How is he?" Al asked.

"I first checked for a heart ailment. I've seen that with kids playing sports from time to time. That wasn't it. I did a full CBC and nothing showed itself. Then I noticed your son was suffering from lockjaw."

"Lockjaw?" Zoe said.

"Yeah, it's a sure sign of botulism poisoning."

"What?" Al said, incredulous.

"Your son has been exposed to botulinum. Did he eat from one of those food carts on the field?"

"No," Zoe insisted.

"What does this mean, Doctor?"

"Well, I've put him on a proper course of treatment, and he should be fine."

Al was breathing again. Dr. Dunn rose, and Zoe stepped forward and stumbled. Al reached out, missing her, but Dr. Dunn grabbed her before she hit the floor. Dr. Dunn at first thought she had merely fainted from all the stress.

"She okay, Doctor?" Al said.

"Have you guys eaten recently?"

"No, not really," Al answered.

"I'm going to check her in."

Dr. Dunn checked Zoe in while Al and Carla, their daughter, waited. An hour later, Dr. Dunn returned and found Al.

"Mr. Munsen, your wife is also suffering from botulism poisoning."

"What?"

"I know. It's inexplicable. But the tests bear it out. "

Al had been feeling gradually weaker in the last hour. Carla had curled up asleep in his lap and looked to Dr. Dunn.

"I'm sick and so's my daughter."

Dr. Dunn's examination revealed they were getting gradually weaker. It seemed as though the whole Munsen family had the same symptoms.

"Nurse!" Dr. Dunn barked.

A nurse ran up.

"Yes."

"Get these people a room!"

CHAPTER 10

Dr. Dunn had the whole Munsen family in his charge, but without any clear idea as to the source of the sickness, it could be weeks until they would recover enough to help them. He feared some local eatery had infected them and fully expected a rush of victims in the coming hours. But the victims never came. Dunn checked the other hospitals in the area, and there were no other botulism outbreaks.

Dr. Dunn suspected the botulinum had to be in the Munsen home. He picked up the phone in his office and called April Friedman, the head of the local health department. She answered the phone brightly, but when she heard Dr. Dunn's voice she became curt. April had been his nurse before she landed the job in the health department. Dr. Dunn was hard on everyone but especially hard on nurses.

"April."

"Dr. Dunn, how can I help you?" she asked coldly.

He knew he'd been difficult when she worked for him, and she was the type to make him pay for it. He was sure she kept him on the line longer than necessary. Shallow, spiteful woman. Did she think everything was about her? There were lives at stake.

"Can you please hurry," he said, using the word "please" in an effort to soften her up. He was unaccustomed to being polite, especially with underlings. Dunn went on to describe the Munsen family and their dire situation. He gave April the Munsen's address and the information necessary to fill out the AB-28 impact report required before an investigation. It seemed to take forever.

"I'll get back to you as soon as I examine the Munsen house," April said.

When April got back to her office after examining the Munsen house, she called Dunn.

"Yes?"

"Dr. Dunn."

"Yes."

"We examined the Munsen house."

"And?"

"First off, it was immaculate. This lady's the best housekeeper I've ever seen. Textbook cleanliness. Everything was sealed properly. All meats were neatly wrapped and frozen. She even wrote dates on the food. We searched the garbage. No containers from fast food places. And she had a bottle of Purell in practically every room."

"Hand sanitizer?"

"Yeah. Talked to the neighbors. Mrs. Munsen is known as a clean freak. So you wasted my afternoon, Doctor."

There was a long pause on the other end.

"This is where you say, 'I'm sorry. I was wrong, April.'"

"I don't have time for verbal volleyball. This is serious."

"Maybe they ate in your hospital cafeteria."

"Very funny. Thanks for your help."

Dr. Dunn hung up.

Dr. Dunn looked into the Munsen ward and checked their progress. They were stable, but something kept nagging at him. He just didn't like the idea of a whole family hit by botulism. It didn't feel right. Deep down in a place within himself he wrestled with the thought that he needed to open the Book.

The Book was a set of rules that he had put together after September 11. It was a book of procedures on how to deal with bioterrorism threats. Several other department heads had deemed The Book alarmist. Dr. Dunn had received a lot of flack, but Dr. Dunn thought it was necessary. He researched and developed the protocols that should be followed in the case there was a bio-threat. The Book had never been used. The Book, though Dunn never would have admitted it, had become an embarrassment.

He entered the storage closet adjacent to his office and found the Book. He grabbed it and sat down at his desk. Dunn closed the door and methodically thumbed through the procedure manual.

He had been explicit in his steps. He flipped to the heading of unusual outbreaks and looked to the subchapter on botulism. The instructions were clear. If a multiple outbreak occurred of any of the diseases or toxins listed, the doctor in charge was obliged to call the CDC counterterrorism unit.

Dr. Dunn sat back in his chair. It had been nine years since September 11, and the panic that was in the air then had certainly subsided. He wondered if the Book was an overreaction. He eyed his phone and sighed. A botulism outbreak wasn't that big a deal, but he had put the rules in the Book and gotten the board to approve them. If anything did go wrong, everyone would be blaming him for not following his very own procedures.

He flipped to the back of the Book and found a phone number. He dialed and waited until a woman with a laconic southern drawl answered the phone.

"CDC, Atlanta. How may I direct your call?"

"Counterterrorism, please."

"Is this an alert call?"

Dr. Dunn paused, knowing his next words could either haunt him or make him a hero.

"Sir, is this an alert call?" the operator repeated in a flatter, more serious tone.

"Uh, yes, yes it is. Could you put me through?"

"What level, sir?"

"Level?"

"Red, orange , or yellow?"

Dunn wiped his mouth and figured you were always safe when you took the middle view of things.

"Orange."

"Orange Alert. Hold on, please."

While he waited, he shook his head to himself. He cursed himself for putting the Book together. A voice answered on the other end.

"This is Dr. Root."

CHAPTER 11

Dr. Root had been meeting resistance with Dr. Lussier over Dr. Dave Richard's future with the CDC. It was actually less resistance and more avoidance. Root had friends in high places, and Lussier wasn't enamored with the idea of a showdown with him. He knew Root was a nice guy who didn't seem to be angling for his job, but he also knew when you anger a nice guy he can suddenly turn. Lussier had learned that nice guys often repress their anger, and you never wanted to be on the receiving end of that.

Dr. Root was walking down the hallway, talking to his wife Emily on his cell phone about the plans for their daughter's bat mitzvah. It was two years off, and it seemed like Emily was jumping the gun. Emily insisted that nothing was further from the truth. They had to nail down dates early. As Emily got more excited, Root caved in and told her to run all the costs by him before she did anything. Emily agreed and hung up.

Root found himself at the top of the basement steps of the CDC and headed down with a thin file in hand. The basement was musty and needed a good cleaning. His trips down here were rare. If he needed Dave he'd call him up to his office. But this time he didn't want anyone to know their business.

He rounded a corner and found Dave's office door open. The hallway was dark, and only the light from Dave's office illuminated the corridor. It was a power-saving move started by a memo by a junior employee trying to make a name for himself.

Dr. Root knocked on the edge of the door, and Dave looked up from an Internet chess game. Root stepped in and took a seat on a cluttered couch that barely fit in the office.

"How're you doing?" Root asked.

"Things are kind of slow. You know."

"You beat the computer?"

"A draw."

"Impressive," Root said while opening a file and handing it to Dave. Dave looked it over quickly without looking up.

"Botulism? What do you want me to do with this?" Dave looked up at Root, who had taken out a clipboard and was writing up a travel order on a pink sheet with a carbon underneath it.

"Got an outbreak I want you to look into. It's in Hope, Arkansas."

"Seems kind of pedestrian." Dr. Root was just short of giving him a scolding look, and Dave immediately picked up on it. "But I'll take pedestrian."

"Look," Dr. Root started. "You're not doing yourself any favors by sitting in your cave playing Internet chess all day. This is a simple assignment. I want you to go there and do a solid report of the situation and come home. I need to prove to Lussier that you have…value."

"So you found a simple task I wasn't likely to screw up." Dr. Root blanched and shook his head.

"I didn't say that. I know how capable you are, and you know that."

"It's everybody else."

"Right."

"I know," Dave said retreating. "Thanks. I appreciate this."

Dr. Root handed Dave the pink travel voucher. These were like gold because it allowed the recipient to fly to any part of the country and live on the federal dime for up to two weeks. All Dave had to do was to bring the voucher upstairs to the payroll department, and he'd be issued a special CDC debit card.

"When do I leave?" Dave asked.

"Immediately. Look, it wouldn't hurt if you were, well, out of sight while your review is discussed."

"Sure. Thanks again."

Dr. Root headed back up the musty stairs as Dave looked at his voucher and the file. He was grateful he finally had something to do.

The Little Rock flight was uneventful. Dave used his upgrade points to fly first class. The food was better, but he forgot that they served champagne like water. The guy next to him, a Texas businessman, drank for the whole journey.

"You're not drinking?"

"No," Dave said.

"Aw. Come on. No one likes to drink alone. Besides, why the hell else do you fly in first class?"

"Sorry, I gotta pass."

The Texan drank half a bottle, then piped up again.

"Come on boy, I got the stewardess to crack open the good stuff. It's on me."

"I can't."

"You got something against rednecks?"

"No, look, I'm an alcoholic, you got it?"

"Aw, hell, so am I but you don't see it getting me down. Trouble with you is you gotta embrace your weaknesses."

"That's the problem. I've had mine in a beer mug for years," Dave said, stifling anger. Even before Dave went on the wagon Dave had decided that drinking and flying didn't mix. A few years back he got on a flight and drank himself into such a stupor that he woke up in bed with a plump Asian girl in her flat in London. Dave didn't remember the flight or landing in Heathrow and absolutely had no idea how he ended up in the bed of the zaftig Vietnamese girl with an unintelligible cockney accent. He had intended to travel to South Dakota to a conference and ended up on the other side of the world. It hadn't stopped him from drinking, but it stopped him from drinking before he flew.

The 757 touched down at Little Rock National Airport around two o'clock in the afternoon. Dave arranged a car rental from Hertz. The car was waiting with the keys inside it. Dave engaged the GPS and soon found himself in Dr. Dunn's office.

Dunn looked uncomfortable as he went over the charts. Dave made copious notes. This report had to be perfect. His future was depending on it. He reviewed the activities and movements of the Munsen family, and just like everyone else, he drew a blank.

Dave went the extra mile and paid a visit to the immaculate Munsen family home to see if there was anything the local authorities had missed. They had been thorough. But his great gift had always been to be able to find things that others could not. He had to bring his gift to the table.

No matter how hard he tried, the mystery of how the family became infected was no closer to being solved.

Dave padded up the plush-carpeted stairs into the master bedroom. It's not likely that you'd get botulism from anything that was in a person's bedroom, but he wanted to cover everything.

He inspected the room, but he didn't think there was anything here that could shed light on the incident. He was about to leave when he spotted a discarded airline ticket sticking out of a small wastebasket. He reached in and retrieved four Jet Blue tickets. Dave opened the tickets and saw the Munsens had just come back from New York City. It was possible that they had eaten something on the flight that had made them sick.

Dave got into his Hertz Prius and drove back to the Little Rock airport. He had to check every possibility. He headed over to the Jet Blue counter and showed his CDC badge. The manager of the office, a bland-looking, asexual woman, came out quickly and was very accommodating. Dave told her of his fear that the Munsen family was sickened by a meal on one of their flights.

The manager, tense at first, relaxed when Dave mentioned food. She assured him there was no way that the Munsens could have gotten botulism from their flight.

"Anything is possible," Dave told her diplomatically.

"But we don't serve meals."

"Oh."

"I think you're barking up the wrong tree," she said dismissively.

"Sorry, I didn't mean to accuse. I'm just exploring every possibility."

Dave was disappointed. He thought he had put the pieces together. It would have made his report impressive, but that wasn't to be. He thanked her for her time, and she smiled politely. He hoped she wouldn't complain to the CDC, but he was pleasant throughout and he had backed off when she shot down his theory.

Dave got back into his rental car and dialed up the CDC and Dr. Root.

"How's Little Rock?" Dr. Root teased.

"Makes a great vacation spot."

"How'd it go?"

"Pretty routine. Unfortunately, we still have no idea how they came in contact with botulinum," Dave said.

"Write up the report and drop a copy off at the FBI office in Little Rock. It's Homeland Security formalities you gotta follow. Everybody's gotta know what everybody else is doing."

"Sure. I'll get right on that."

Dave hung up and drove over to his motel. He spent the better part of the afternoon writing and rewriting the report. He was very detailed in his breakdown of the Munsen incident and looked at the report proudly, feeling he had actually accomplished something for the first time in a long time. He didn't find the source, but he did a credible, by-the-book job for a change.

Dave called the FBI office and was directed to Paula Mushari, who gave him directions to the office. Dave drove down and parked on the street. He walked in with the report in hand and found Paula Mushari in her office.

Paula was thirty years old with long, dark black hair; slim, but with muscular arms. She was Lebanese and had an accent that went in and out. Clearly, she was trying to minimize it. Dave noticed a dog-eared book on eliminating accents on her desk.

Paula looked up at Dave, smiled, and offered her hand.

"I'm Special Agent Mushari."

"Dr. Dave Richards. CDC. Got a report for you." Dave handed her the file and she sat down. As she read, she indicated that Dave take a seat. Paula read the whole report quickly and looked at Dave.

"Not much here," she said.

"Just following protocol."

"Sometimes following protocol pays off. I've seen it happen before. That is weird though; a whole family coming down with the same infection. You ever run across this?"

"Can't say that I have."

"You work out of Atlanta?"

"Yeah.

"Don't have an accent."

"Yeah, well, that's where the job is."

"Let you in on a little secret. I'm not from Little Rock." Dave laughed.

Dave offered her his cell phone number in case there was a need for follow-up. They shook hands, and he headed back to his car. Dave wondered if he had done everything he could. In the old days he would follow his instincts until he found an answer, but now he was acting like a mediocre civil servant. He figured it was safer.

Dave had already checked out of the motel and planned he'd take an earlier flight home.

Dave returned his rental car. He checked his bags, sat by his gate, and read the paper. He was a little stung when that FBI agent had commented that there wasn't much there. But the truth was, it was a dry affair. A family got sick, and there were no clues as to why. He wondered if this excursion would save his job.

The United counter announced the boarding of Flight 234 to Atlanta. Dave got up and headed for the gate, tossing his paper in the trash. There was an Adam Sandler movie on the flight back, and he was looking forward to seeing it. He wouldn't be reading, so he didn't need the *Arkansas Democrat*.

Dave had just handed his ticket to a boarding agent when his cell phone rang. Dave looked at the phone and saw the FBI was trying to call him. He got out of line and answered the phone.

"Hello."

"This is Agent Mushari."

"Hi, is there something wrong with the report?"

"No, no, nothing like that," she said quickly. "Where are you?"

"I'm at Little Rock Airport about to board."

"Don't get on the plane. I need you to stay."

Dave didn't like the idea of a law enforcement official telling him not to leave town. He felt guilty even though he knew he hadn't done anything.

"Uh, sure, what's up?"

"I just got a call from a Dr. Dunn. He's been trying to get a hold of you."

"Why?"

"Another family got sick in Hope, Arkansas." Dave stepped away from the gate to get better reception. "Another family got botulism?"

"No," Paula said. "The plague. Bubonic plague." Dave went over to the ticket counter and threw his ticket and his CDC badge down in front of the counter attendant.

"The plague? Is he sure?"

"Dead sure. Listen: meet me at the family's house. I'll call back with the address." Paula hung up and Dave told the woman at United to get his bags off the plane. She said she wasn't sure she could. He informed the woman at the United counter the FBI needed him to stay. The flight was delayed by a half an hour as his bags were retrieved. Dave took the time to track down Dr. Root, who was just finishing dinner at home.

"Are you back?"

"No, I gotta stay longer. We got a bubonic plague outbreak."

"Where?"

"Uh, well, same town. Hope."

"The plague and botulism in the same small town? What the hell's that about?"

"It's not possible. That's what it's about."

"It's gotta be a misdiagnosis."

"Don't know. Met the doctor. He's pretty sharp. Well trained."

"Okay, well, look, Dave, keep me updated hourly. And try to keep this quiet. We don't need a panic."

Dave hung up and went back to Hertz. He rented a Mustang and headed out to find out what the devil was going on in Hope.

CHAPTER 12

Dr. Dunn was reading about the Black Death on the Internet in his office. The first pandemic was in around AD 541 in Constantinople. Another outbreak occurred in AD 588 that killed around twenty-five million people in Gaul, now known as France. The most notable incident began in central Asia and rolled to Europe by the 1340s. Dunn figured it must have seemed like the end of the world when the disease erased seventy-five million lives. A nurse popped her head in.

"Doctor."

"Yes."

She looked at his computer screen and saw the title, "The Black Death."

"Don't worry. That was a long time ago, and we have French bacteriologist Alexandre Yersin to thank for isolating the bacterium."

"Still plague, Doctor."

"I know. Never ran across it in my career."

"The patients have started their courses. I'm having trouble getting nurses to…"

"Work near them?"

"Yes."

"That's unacceptable. Everyone will go on the treatment who's dealing with the case."

"I've had a few not show up for work."

"Tell the chief of nurses that I want to speak to her. There's a public trust here that needs to be adhered to. If there needs to be a change made, I'll insist on it."

"Yes, Doctor."

Dr. Dunn had the Kellogg family sealed in an airtight hospital suite. He'd made sure that everyone who'd been in contact with the family took the proper series of prophylactic antibiotics. He chose ciprofloxacin—500 mg two times a day for ten days for all those at risk, including himself.

Dr. Dunn was monitoring the Kellogg family all morning. The fevers were still high, but he was confident that the intravenous administration of the antibiotic gentamicin in both the adults and children would break the plague's back. He'd never had to treat it before, but he was handling it by the book, as that was his style.

Dr. Yoav Gerson, the sixty-year-old chief of surgery walked toward Dr. Dunn. They shook hands. Dr. Dunn looked back to his chart, reviewing the latest CBC tests on the father, Eldon Kellogg.

"Dr. Dunn," he said in his sharp Israeli accent. "A moment, please." Dr. Dunn closed the chart and let it hang by his side.

"Yes."

"Do you have a copy of the procedures? The bioterror procedures?" Dr. Dunn smiled. Dr. Gerson wasn't around when the procedures book was written. He hadn't been one of the many doctors who had accused him of being alarmist. Dunn quickly surmised that all the other doctors were too embarrassed to ask him for the Book. But Gerson didn't care. He was obviously glad there had been some forethought.

"It's in my office," Dunn said. "I guess we'd better make copies and finally get it distributed."

"Excellent idea. I think we should have a meeting with all the department heads tonight. You could go through all the working parts, so to speak."

Dr. Dunn had a buzz of self-satisfaction. He nodded gravely.

Dr. Dunn and Dr. Gerson headed toward Dunn's office. Dunn felt vindicated. But he wished he could be at the Kellogg house being part of the investigation. But Dr. Dunn had his hands full here taking care of the Munsen and Kellogg cases.

They reached Dr. Dunn's office and he picked up the Book and handed it to Dr. Gerson. Gerson smiled and told him to keep his schedule open for a staff meeting.

Dunn's phone rang, and he picked it up. At first there was a digitizing sound on the other end. He couldn't make out the voice.

"Hello. You're garbled."

"Is that better?" Dave Richards said. Dunn could tell Dave was driving from the sounds of passing traffic.

"Dr. Richards, have you gotten to the house yet?"

"Not yet. Got lost. I'll be there in a few minutes. How're the patients doing?"

Dr. Dunn gave Dave a rundown on each patient. The mother was in the worst shape. She had bite-like red bumps on her skin and seemed to be the furthest along. Dr. Dunn felt it was too early to comment on their collective morbidity. He wasn't sure how long they had been exposed.

"Well, hopefully I'll find the source at the house."

"I hope so, too. Keep me updated."

"I will."

Dave's Mustang was just around the corner from the Kellogg house. Dave hung up the phone and turned down Kelso Road. Police cars, fire trucks, and Arkansas Health Department vehicles blocked the small street. Panicked residents were being urged out of their homes by overwhelmed small-town cops.

Dave parked his car and walked toward the Kellogg house. It had already been tented, and a sign was planted in front. "No Admittance by Order of the Arkansas Health Department."

April Friedman was in a tizzy. She had been made team leader only two months ago, and now she was sitting on the biggest crisis the state had ever encountered. She was being pummeled with questions that she didn't have answers to. But April always rose to the occasion.

Dave approached her, extending his hand. April looked up, spotted the CDC badge around his neck, and looked relieved.

"You're Dr. Richards?"

"Yeah."

"April Friedman. Arkansas Health. You sure got here fast."

"I was already here for the Munsen business." April nodded and marched over to a makeshift dressing room.

"I assume you want to go in."

"That's the plan," Dave said as he entered the tent that was packed with Tyvek HAZMAT suits. They were thick and bulky with oxygen backpacks. They were state of the art. He smiled when he saw Paula Mushari zipping up her suit before donning the face mask.

"You made it," Paula said.

Before he could answer, April Friedman grabbed one of the turquoise suits off a table and was holding it toward Dave.

"Get this on. You ever worn one? Do I need to show you how to put it on?"

Dave calmed the nervous April and donned the HAZMAT suit. April sat down on a plastic chair and wiped sweat from her brow. She jumped up, realizing that she needed to check on the decontamination setup.

Dave watched Paula seal her helmet. Dave did likewise and then did a radio check. They agreed they could hear each other clearly. They stepped out of the tent and walked over to the Kellogg house.

Dave felt invigorated. He felt as though he was part of something important for the first time in a long time. Drinking had taken him off track for what seemed like an eternity. As Dave heard the loud suction sound of the breathing apparatus pumping oxygen into his lungs, he remembered why the path to the CDC was so important to him. It was for times like this. Despite the tragedy that had befallen the Kellogg family, Dave felt like he was on an adventure. He was on a hunt for the truth. He was certain that he had stumbled onto something extraordinary, and not only was it going get his mental juices flowing again, but it would quite likely save his job. Something flashed through his brain at that moment. Dave realized that he hadn't thought about tequila for most of the morning. Every day since he'd been on the wagon, he would remember and savor Patrón. But Patrón hadn't crossed mind since he got the call from Paula to meet him at the Kellogg house. He was on a different high.

Paula broke the seal into the home and hurried Dave in. Paula sealed it behind her and they entered. The first thing Dave noticed was a simple painting of Jesus in the foyer. A crown of light was emanating from his head, and it made Dave feel uncomfortable. He was raised Episcopalian, and religion was never on his sleeve. He noted many religious icons throughout the house and wondered how a family that embraced God so deeply could have such bad luck. Paula's voice crackled in Dave's earpiece.

"I don't know what to look for."

Dave had to turn his whole body to face her. The helmet restricted his movement, and he saw Paula standing by the entrance into the dining room.

"Rat droppings would be a dead giveaway. Since it is carried by rat fleas," Dave said.

"I've gotta find a dead flea?" Paula asked.

Dave and Paula looked through the kitchen and in the basement. They covered every inch of the house and turned up nothing. Their search went on for several hours. Dave took samples and placed them in an airtight kit, carefully cataloging everything.

Paula suggested they check the garbage in the garage. Dave agreed. Dave looked at his air gauge and realized that he had only forty-five minutes left.

"Let's be quick about it."

Dave and Paula entered the cluttered garage and began their search. Time was running out, but they needed to find a clear answer. Dave was getting frustrated. Nothing. Just like the Munsen house. Dave got on all fours, desperately trying to find a rat dropping. The Kelloggs weren't as clean at the Munsens, but clearly rats weren't the culprits.

Paula found a waste can and cracked it open looking for telltale signs of rat feces. She cleared through the trash, found a ticket, and held it up, looking it over. Dave looked around and saw the ticket and grabbed it out of Paula's hand. It was a Jet Blue ticket. The travel dates were the same as the Munsens'. An alarm buzzer went off in Paula's helmet first. She'd been in her suit a little longer than Dave. His suit soon started buzzing, warning of the impending oxygen cutoff.

"We've only got five minutes."

"I know. I think this was a bust."

"Maybe you've got something in your sample case." Paula indicated a kit with CDC emblazoned on the side.

"Maybe."

Dave and Paula headed to the front door, navigating awkwardly in the bulky suits. Paula opened the seal that took them back outside, and they crossed through. Paula resealed it behind her, and they rushed over to the decontamination tent that had been set up to the right side of the house. They hooked into another oxygen source while they waited to be scrubbed down.

After they got out of the suits, Dave noticed Paula seemed uneasy.

"You okay?"

"Hate those suits. Make me sweat like a pig."

"Yeah, that was a rough five hours."

"I have some clothes in my car."

"Go ahead."

Dave watched Paula slip into her car while he chugged a bottle of water. A few minutes later she reappeared in jeans and a T-shirt. She no longer looked like a typical FBI agent. She just looked like the girl next door with her hair tied in a ponytail. In the short time she'd known Dr. Dave Richards, she realized that she didn't need to act like a tough agent around him. She was glad, since tough took a lot of energy and she was bone tired. Paula looked around for Dave and saw him standing in the yard of the house opposite the Kelloggs'.

Dave was looking at the Jet Blue ticket, now sealed in a plastic pouch. Paula came up to him and took the ticket away from him. Dave looked at her, annoyed.

"You think this means something?"

"Yeah, I found one of these Jet Blue tickets with the same travel dates in the Munsen house. Checked with Jet Blue and came to a dead end."

"They don't serve meals."

"Does everybody know that?"

"Pretty much."

Dave sat on the curb pensively and hoped that he could figure out what he had missed. He wanted to recapture some of the enthusiasm and passion he'd had in his youth, when answers seemed to come easily to him.

Paula sat next to him and looked up to see all eyes were on them: the local cops, the state police, the firemen, and the Arkansas Health Department. Dave noticed, too, and nudged Paula.

"Just nod and look intelligent." Paula noticed the attention and then nodded and attempted to look very intelligent.

Paula whispered to him, "Why am I doing this?"

Dave whispered back,"I don't want any of them to know we don't have a clue."

Paula laughed and said, "That's how all investigations start. But we've got something now. Both families were on the same flight."

"But we've got two different diseases. If it were just recirculated air…" Dave started.

"…there might be one disease," Paula finished. Paula stood and ambled down to a cow-shaped mailbox and looked back at him.

"You were in the Munsen house. There any other similarities?"

Dave rose and crossed to her, recounting his investigation of the Munsen home. Dave paused in mid thought. Paula sensed he was onto something.

"Those Jesus paintings. The Munsens had them, too."

Paula frowned, walking up to Dave and shaking her head. "It's the South. Everybody's house has wall-to-wall Jesus paintings."

"I'll bet yours doesn't." Dave smiled. "What do you have on your walls?"

"No picture of Mohammed, that's for sure. It's a Muslim no-no. I favor Hockney."

"Right." Dave took back the ticket and saw a panicked neighbor hustling out of her house with two pink suitcases. They matched her pink stretch pants. She hurried down the stone path from her front yard and tripped. Dave caught her and helped her up. She thanked him and introduced herself as Shirley. She noticed the CDC badge.

"You're with the government?"

"Yeah."

"How are the Kelloggs? I just don't know what I'd do if anything happened to them. Vivian Kellogg and I have been bridge partners for ten years. You can't get what they've got by sharing cards, can you?" Dave shook his head and handed her her suitcase.

"They're in good hands," Dave assured her.

Shirley went back to get her shoe that had fallen off. She slipped it back on and then looked to Paula. Shirley noticed the airline ticket and shook her head.

"They'd been so excited." Shirley looked up at Dave and Paula. "The trip to New York. The church put it together. They were going to see the cathedral and then go to a big conference, I think. None of them had ever been to New York City before."

Shirley started toward her car and put the suitcases in the trunk of her Volvo. Paula followed Shirley but stopped when she was about to get in the driver's seat. Paula put her hand on the car door firmly. Shirley seemed a little put off by Paula's mild aggressiveness.

"We need to ask you a few questions."

"A few questions? What about? I need to get out of here before I end up in the hospital like them." Dave moved up between Shirley and Paula.

"This church group," Dave started. "Did the Munsens go with them?"

"You didn't know that?"

"No, ma'am."

"Well, you need to be more thorough. What do we pay you for anyway?"

Paula moved up to Shirley.

"Can you tell us anything else about the church group?"

"Well, of course. A whole passel of families went on the church-group trip to New York. You didn't know that?"

"We didn't know it was a church group. Which church?"

"The Church of the Divinity on Main Street. Do I have to show you a map?"

"No, ma'am," Paula said.

"And excuse me, I'm not a ma'am. I'm thirty-seven, and I have a boyfriend, thank you very much."

Paula looked at Dave, and they both realized that they'd finally made some headway. They questioned Shirley for another fifteen minutes and took notes. She didn't have any other revelations for them, but she'd already helped them out in a big way.

Dave and Paula could feel the eyes on them, and they disappeared behind Shirley's house for some privacy. Paula sat on a kids' swing while Dave paced.

"We should get the results from the samples you took tonight."

"All the results will be negative." Paula got up off the swing and walked up to him.

"Because they were infected in New York," Paula realized. Dave nodded. Paula's face twisted up, puzzled. He could see something wasn't fitting together for her.

"How could two families in the same church group get exposed to two different deadly diseases?"

"Beats the hell out of me," Dave said. "Unless they went on a tour of a bioweapons facility. That's hardly likely."

"Last time I looked, they didn't offer tours," Paula added. "Look, there's something up here."

Dave actually knew the mathematical odds of the two families being infected but chose not to share them so as not to sound like know-it-all. It was a challenge because he was a know-it-all. He had more useless information in his head than he'd care to admit.

Paula looked at Dave. First she held her tongue because she was worried what he'd think of her if she voiced her fears. He didn't seem judgmental, so she decided to take a chance.

"Don't you think this feels, well, terrorism related?" She instantly regretted the words the minute they came out of her mouth. But Dave didn't look at her like she was green and overeager. It had crossed his mind, too. Things like this don't happen unless someone wants them to.

"It's frankly what I was thinking, but it's only a hunch. And we need more than an educated guess before we push the panic button."

"You're saying we need the smoking gun," Paula said, glad they were on the same page.

"Yeah. I mean, I don't know about your bosses, but if you tell mine there's a killer whale in the water, they won't believe it until it bites them in the ass."

Paula smiled. "I think we've got the same bosses."

"We need a lot more information," he started. "The trail leads to New York, and that's where we need to go."

"If we follow where the church group went, maybe we'll find the point where they got infected," Paula added.

They heard footsteps coming around the corner and looked up to see April Friedman. She tentatively came into to the backyard and waved. Clearly, she had been elected by the state troopers, the local cops, and the firemen to find out what was going on.

"So what's the deal? Do we have to burn down the neighborhood or what?" April asked, trying to remain light. Neither Dave nor Paula smiled, and April worried for a moment that was exactly what they had to do.

Dave beckoned her over, and she edged up to them. April kept sifting her fingers through her dry, matted hair.

"In all likelihood the plague didn't start at the house. I'm betting all the tests are going to be negative. Figure the residents will be able to move back in tomorrow."

"Thank God. Closing down dirty restaurants is more my style. Handling a pandemic? Well, not so much."

"Oh, we're not out of the woods. You got a notepad?"

"Yeah," she said, pulling one out of her back pocket. She'd forgotten a pen, and Paula handed her one.

"Here's where we need your help," Dave said. "These two families were on the same church-group trip, and we think that's the key. You guys need to get every name on the list and have them tested for plague and botulism. Now I want all the officers involved to wear masks, gloves, the whole deal."

April wrote down everything Dave said. She ran back around to the men in front who were awaiting their next move. She spilled out the orders, and they all listened and hung on her every word. The chief listened intently and quickly jumped into action. The state troopers were sent to the Church of the Divinity to get the list of the members of the church group that had been on the trip. The local cops and the firemen knew a dozen or so friends that had gone on the New York trip and fanned out to connect with them. Soon police cars raced away from the scene, sirens blazing. Dave and Paula walked back toward their cars.

"You have access to a jet?" Dave said.

"For emergencies."

"What do you think this is?"

Paula nodded and said, "I guess we're going to New York City."

"I guess we are," Dave said. They got in their cars and headed back to the FBI office in Little Rock.

PART TWO

DARKNESS RISING

CHAPTER 13

The Henrys didn't live in Hope. They lived in Texarkana but went on the trip to New York because one family had dropped out, and the tickets were paid for. Martha Henry had thought it was a coup. She liked the idea of her children, Kelsey and Robbie, seeing something other than the bland surroundings of Texarkana. Martha had seen much of the world before and during college. Her father was a major in the Army, and she traveled the world with him. Martha married her husband, Bert, who was from Texarkana, and they settled there. He had a good job selling insurance with Mutual of Omaha, and life had turned out well for them. But Martha was in the kind of turmoil only a mother can feel when something isn't quite right with her child. Kelsey was twelve and had stopped eating a few days back. Martha was afraid that Kelsey was suffering from anorexia, so she had checked out a stack of books on the subject from the public library. Martha had followed some of the guidance offered in the books, but nothing seemed to change Kelsey's condition. Martha learned that there was a therapist a few towns over that specialized in this disorder. They had a session a day for three days in a row, and the therapist pronounced that Kelsey was not suffering from anorexia nervosa. He didn't know what was wrong with her, but she didn't have anorexia.

It wasn't until dinner one night, when Bert placed a glass of water in front of Kelsey, that the pieces began to come together. Kelsey's eyes widened in terror at the sight of the glass of water. She began screaming, recoiling from the glass.

Martha looked at Bert for answers. Bert couldn't help but think that some madness had befallen his daughter. He remembered that his aunt had gone mad and was institutionalized in a facility in Dayton, Ohio. He didn't dare suggest that to Martha. He just froze. Bert was a decent man, but an uncomplicated one.

Martha went to Reverend McConnell for solace. She desperately needed guidance and got less than what she'd hoped for. He was kind and understanding, but in the end unhelpful. He noticed that she was sweating and offered his handkerchief to wipe her brow. Martha was getting feverish; something was wrong with her. She stared out into space, glassy eyed, as Reverend McConnell tried to get her attention.

"Martha. Martha. Martha, are you okay?"

Martha Henry just stared straight ahead, unaware of where she was.

"Martha." Martha looked around, coming out of her fog.

"Oh, sorry. I guess I'm not myself."

"That's understandable."

The reverend helped her to her car. She got in and drove off. She opened the window, hoping the cool breeze would help clear her head.

CHAPTER 14

Paula Mushari looked out the window of the FBI jet and saw the great expanse that was America. Paula was privately thrilled that she was on an official case with potentially deep implications. Until September 11 she had planned on a career in real estate. Paula was a very attractive woman, but after the towers fell she wasn't seen as "that cute girl" anymore. She was seen as an "Arab woman." This prejudice elevated her anger toward the terrorists. Paula remembered reading about how the Japanese Americans in World War II had joined the Army to prove their loyalty to the country that had put them in prison camps. She had toyed with joining the Army but joined the FBI instead. When people saw she was with the FBI, there was no question of where her allegiance lay. She gained back the respect she had lost. She wasn't just the "Arab woman" anymore; she was Special Agent Paula Mushari.

She wanted to fight terrorism, but she found herself not in Washington DC or New York City. She was assigned to Little Rock, Arkansas. She had been assigned to white-collar crime. She was good at it, but it wasn't where her heart was. She couldn't help but wonder if the olive color of her skin had relegated her to this assignment. She asked her friend Anna Tubbs, an African American FBI agent, how she could tame the doubts they must have about her.

Anna told her that though they want Muslims in the FBI, there are still some men at the higher levels of the agency who would never trust one. This only increased Paula's resolve to crack a big terrorism case so there would be no question about her patriotism.

But her dream had eluded her. Though she caught the eye of numerous men, she was married to the FBI. She was willing to make the sacrifice. She looked over at Dave Richards and pondered if somehow he was the key to her success.

Paula looked around the jet's interior. It seated twelve and was very quiet. Dave looked over to her.

"I could get used to this," he said.

"Don't. The cost of jet fuel is murder."

"There any snacks?"

"In the fridge." Paula went over and opened it, revealing a treasure trove of goodies. "Lotta choices," she said, considering.

"I had an Israeli roommate at Dartmouth. He had a saying."

Dave moved over next to Paula, looking in the fridge.

"What was that?"

"If it's free, take two."

"One smart Israeli."

Dave grabbed a candy bar and some peanuts and retreated back to his seat.

Dave started on the candy bar and took in the view. Paula took the time to catch up on paperwork she had to file on the two cases in Hope. Her immediate superior, Gary Hung, sent her off to New York with his blessing. He thought quite a bit of Paula and felt her skills were being squandered in Little Rock. He was glad she finally had an opportunity to show the bureau what she was capable of.

Paula finished typing on her laptop and closed it up. She heard the grinding of the landing gears as they locked into position, and she sensed the jet's descent into Kennedy.

The weather was murky over the skyline of New York. It seemed to take an eternity for the plane to break through the clouds. Paula pressed her face against the window like a little kid. It never ceased to amaze her that she was hurtling through the air at five hundred miles an hour. Her eyes widened as New York materialized before her. It was her favorite city and, for the first time, she was visiting on official business.

The plane touched down with only the slightest of bounces. They taxied over to a secluded section of Kennedy and parked.

Dave and Paula stepped out of the plane and were met with the near-deafening whine of numerous throttling jet engines.

A tall, prematurely gray FBI agent named Pearson waved them over to his black Crown Victoria. He offered his hand and gave them both quick handshakes.

"Welcome to New York," he yelled over the deafening thrust of a passing 747. "Do you want to go to the hotel first or meet Father Vincent?" Dave stepped forward and yelled over the engines.

"We got a late start. Let's go see Vincent," Dave said. Dave looked to Paula, who nodded.

Dave and Paula got in the back seat of the unmarked government car and raced out of Kennedy. The ride was quiet; neither Pearson nor the driver tried to make conversation. Paula kept quiet, not wanting to sound like a green agent from the South. New York was the second best posting in the FBI next to Washington DC. She wanted to give off an air of confidence. She put on a pair of sunglasses she'd bought to toughen up her image. She looked over at Dave who held back laughter. She mouthed to him, "What?"

Dave reached up and yanked the dangling price tag from the glasses. Paula blushed and mouthed the words, "Thank you." Dave nodded then tapped her shoulder and pointed outside.

Saint Patrick's Cathedral came into view. It was made of white marble and dominated two city blocks. The cathedral's spires stretched over three hundred feet into the sky. This, of course, paled in comparison to the skyscrapers in the vicinity.

The Crown Victoria pulled up in front of the cathedral as best as it could. There was no place to park, not unusual on the streets in New York.

Pearson looked back at them and said, "We'll circle while you conduct your interview."

Paula nodded and opened the door. She and Dave stepped out and made their way into the cathedral. They found a priest carrying a sacrament case down the center aisle in the middle of the pews. He looked around and asked, "May I help you?"

"We have an appointment with Father Vincent," Paula said.

The priest indicated that they should follow him and crossed to an elevator on the south end of the cathedral. Dave and Paula stepped into the elevator, and they shot up more quickly than expected in a building this old.

"We just had the elevator refurbished. It's got quite a kick to it. Makes you feel like you're headed straight to the Lord." He smiled.

They came off the elevator and found themselves facing Father Vincent's secretary, Helen Cooney. She was about sixty with gray hair, a gray dress, and gray knee socks. She had a faint Irish lilt that she seemed proud of, but it had clearly lost its punch.

"You're the FBI?"

The priest acted a little stunned, not realizing whom he had brought upstairs. Since the sexual abuse scandal, the arrival of law enforcement officers in a Catholic church set off alarm bells with many priests.

When Dave announced he was with the CDC, the Priest appeared to exhale. He turned away, reentered the elevator, and headed back to his business.

Helen rose from her immaculate desk, knocked on the thick wooden door, and opened it. Father Vincent was in his forties and a victim of a perpetual five o'clock shadow. He looked up from a sermon he was editing. He was trying to trim it down; his parishioners had complained about his long-windedness.

"The FBI and the CDC are here Father."

Father Vincent rose up from his seat and crossed to Dave and Paula, ushering them in. "Yes, yes, of course. Dr. Richards and Agent Mushari."

"Thanks for seeing us," Paula said, taking a seat in a thick, leather chair.

"It's so awful about what happened to the Arkansas group; horrible. How are they doing, Doctor?" Father Vincent asked.

Dave sat down, and Father Vincent planted himself at the edge of his desk. Dave started, "The Munsens will be fine, but the Kelloggs have a longer, more difficult path." Father Vincent nodded, headed back around to his chair, and plopped down.

"A devilish affliction. How can Saint Patrick's help the CDC and the FBI?"

"We need to know everything about their trip. We need to know where they went. Where they ate. Where they stayed," Paula said.

"You don't think that these people got sick from Saint Patrick's?"

"I don't know, Father," Dave said. "We need to make a thorough examination of the premises and wherever their itinerary took them."

"How in God's name could the black plague have made its way in here?" Father Vincent said, appalled. "We haven't had a vermin infestation in at least five years. And that's when I started here."

While Father Vincent defended the cleanliness of the cathedral, he pulled out a file and flipped it open. He scanned it, nodded to himself, and then looked up at Dave.

"Dr. Richards, this is an hour-by-hour breakdown of the Arkansas group's travels in New York." Father Vincent handed him the file and sat behind his desk. Dave looked at it and then at the priest.

"I'm surprised how much detailed info you took down." Father Vincent looked uncomfortable and shifted in his seat.

"Our lawyers have advised us that when the church is involved with, well, situations that involve families, children, we have to keep extensive documentation."

Dave and Paula nodded. Father Vincent called Helen Cooney in and asked her to make Xerox copies of the Arkansas group file. Father Vincent rose from his chair and pumped their hands.

"Good luck to you."

"Thank you, Father."

"You just wait by Helen's desk and she'll fix you up."

The thick door closed behind them. They waited in Helen's outer office while she made the copies. Dave paced the floor as the Xerox machine churned out pages, two at a time. The reason they had this detailed information was because of the deviant behavior of some unknown priests. It was an odd confluence that something so vile could end up being so positive for them. Helen reentered and handed them the files.

"Here you are. I hope that helps you."

"It does. Thank you."

They descended back down the elevator and out to the street. They waited for a few minutes for Pearson and the driver to pull up.

Dave and Paula hopped in the car and headed uptown. As they drove, they reviewed the documents. Pearson twisted toward them.

"You want to check into your hotel?" he asked.

"I think we need to follow up on these documents first," Dave said.

Pearson turned back around.

"Where's the first stop?" he asked.

Paula looked at the itinerary.

"The Empire State Building."

The driver took a hard turn, and soon they were at what was now the tallest building in New York: a title reclaimed when the World Trade Center fell.

They followed the journey of the Arkansas group on their tour of the building. Dave and Paula looked for clues but saw nothing. The next stop was the Metropolitan Museum. Again, they combed the art-laden building, but there wasn't anything that stood out. Paula hid her frustration. Paula hadn't intended to see the sights, but that's what their journey was turning into. They moved through throngs of tourists, looking for a hint of something that could have triggered a serious illness. Paula was unnerved by Pearson's stoic silence. She felt like he was laughing to himself, assuming them incompetent. Paula imagined him having a good laugh in the New York bureau's offices the next morning over coffee.

It was getting late, and they had one more stop. It was a midtown-Manhattan mall featuring all the high-end favorites of fashionable shoppers. Dave and Paula searched the mall from end to end. Pearson and the driver opted to get dinner at the food court while Paula and Dave continued on.

Paula sat down on a bench, and Dave looked at her curiously.

"What's wrong?"

"I think we're just kidding ourselves."

"I don't think so," Dave said, scanning the mall for a detail he might have missed.

"Frankly, I feel like an idiot," Paula said.

"Why? Look, there is no chance that two families in the same town could come down with a deadly disease. No chance," Dave said sharply. Then he looked up and felt like a fool himself. He had missed the most obvious evidence. Dave nudged Paula, who came out of her funk when she saw Dave pointing to the surveillance cameras that lined the mall.

Dave and Paula knocked on the door of the watch commander of the mall. His badge said "Curly," and he had the withered look of a retired NYPD flatfoot. Dave and Paula flashed their badges, and he became instantly alert.

"FBI? CDC? What can I do for you?"

"We need to see your tapes," Paula said.

Curly grabbed his belt, which featured a nightstick and mace, and headed down a bland hallway. Dave and Paula kept close to him as they entered a state-of-the-art surveillance room covered with TV screens. A woman in a bulky uniform sat before the TVs, monitoring the shoppers' activity. Curly introduced her as Eve, but she didn't turn around. She kept her eyes fixed on the screens and picked up a walkie-talkie that was lying on the control board.

"Hey, Jones. Those kids are back by the Disney Store. Thought you kicked them out."

"I did," a voice crackled back. "I'll kick 'em out again."

Curly tapped the woman on the shoulder and asked her to retrieve some video files. Paula was thankful they were able to go through hours upon hours of digital recordings in a relatively short time. The days of having to go through stacks of VHS tapes were becoming a thing of the past.

"What dates did you want to check?" Curly asked. Paula rifled through the pages and found the date and the time.

Eve typed the date into the computer, and all the screens popped up at the exact date and time. They watched the screens carefully and spotted the church group entering the mall. Nothing seemed odd about their shopping trip until they stopped and turned a corner that was partially out of view. The group members were talking to a young man who seemed to come in and out of view as he spoke to them. It looked like he was making some kind of pitch. Eventually, other members of the church group got engaged with the young man and disappeared out of the camera's shot.

"What's going on? Have you got an angle so we can see from the other side?"

Eve typed into the console and looked increasingly frustrated. She looked in a logbook that was tucked underneath on a shelf by her legs. She poured over the dates. She shook her head.

"We had a system failure that day."

"System failure?" Paula said.

"The camera covering that section went down that morning."

"How?" Dave asked.

"Someone screwed up the patching in the junction."

"Could it have been tampered with?" Paula said.

"I suppose. But why would anyone tamper with that camera? I mean, there's not much over there. Only some benches and plants."

"And it's a perfect place to do something that you don't want anyone to see," Dave said.

"That guy, can we get a still of him? Can you print it out?"

"Yeah, sure."

"Let's go down there," Dave said.

Dave and Paula rounded the corner that had been unseen by the cameras. It was a waiting area. It was for husbands and boyfriends who dutifully sat while their wives and girlfriends shopped. Dave looked at the wall where the young man had been talking to the families.

"I wonder what was he was talking to them about?" Dave asked.

"Whatever it, was he didn't want any record of it," Paula said.

"You think he tampered with the cameras?"

"It's an awful big coincidence, if you ask me."

Dave took samples from around the area where the families had been talking to the young man. Dave swabbed the floors, walls, every possible surface He sealed the swabs in airtight bags.

"You think he infected them right here? How?"

"No idea."

Curly came down carrying the photo of the young man and handed it to them.

"Thanks," Dave said.

"You need anything else, you know how to get me."

Curly headed back through a secure door. Paula looked at the picture.

"We'll drop it off at the FBI and see what they come up with. Maybe the guy's in the database."

"Make sure the lab pushes to get my sample results."

"I'll stay on them."

Dave and Paula were a little glassy-eyed as Pearson and the driver walked up to them.

"So where are we?" Pearson said.

"Further ahead than when we got here. We need an ID on someone ASAP."

Paula handed over the picture of the young man, and Pearson took it.

"Also, we need these samples analyzed. You may want to call the lab and tell them they're working late tonight," Dave said.

"What did you find?" Pearson asked.

"This might be the source of the infections."

"The mall?"

"Could be," Dave said, heading out the front door.

"We ate in there," Pearson said. Dave looked back at them.

"Then you better get those samples tested sooner than later."

Dave and Paula got in the back seat of the Crown Victoria and were taken to the Holiday Inn. Pearson assured them he'd get the needed answers. The car sped off. Paula looked at Dave.

"What if the tests are positive?"

"Well, we gotta figure out how to close a mall without causing a panic."

"That'll be an interesting trick."

Dave walked into the lobby lugging his bags. He twisted around and looked at Paula.

"You have any allergies to medicine?"

"Not that I know of."

Dave saw an assistant manager crossing through the lobby and stopped him.

"Excuse me. Are there any twenty-four-hour pharmacies near here?"

"Actually, yes, sir. Right up the street, one block."

"Thank you."

Paula looked at Dave, confused. Dave sat down at a couch and pulled out a prescription pad. He started writing.

"What are you doing? Why did you ask if I was allergic to anything?"

"Well, since there's a possibility we were in an area where bubonic plague was, we might want to start a course of precautionary antibiotics."

"You're sure?"

"Not at all, but I think it's our best bet."

"So we might have been exposed to plague?"

"Don't worry. You're in good hands. You want to see my diploma?"

Paula grabbed the prescription. She handed him her bag.

"I'm going to fill this."

Paula headed back outside and disappeared from view. Dave headed up to the front desk to check in.

CHAPTER 15

Abrams Preschool was a modest facility. The teachers were kind and genuinely felt the child's growth was paramount. Politics was never an issue among the teachers and the staff. The child was what mattered.

Darcy Mellon was a twenty-five-year-old, mousy-haired young woman who had a voice so cute she could have done voices for cartoons. She had a class of fifteen five-year-olds, and she had just finished going over their ABCs.

"All right, class. Guess what?"

They all yelled, "What?" in unison.

"You've been so good today that I'm going to give you fifteen minutes of 'me' time."

The kids squealed with delight. "Me time" was time when the kids could play in class and do whatever they liked. The classroom was filled with plenty of fun distractions for a five-year-old and, generally, they all played well with one another.

While the kids played ball or cracked that Big Bird puzzle that they hadn't been able to figure out, Darcy sat at her small desk and started doing some of her bills. When she declared "me time" she was also declaring it for herself.

Justin Younger, a pinkish, cherubic boy, was enamored with banging wooden pegs into wooden holes with a wooden hammer. He delighted in the noise and in his sense of accomplishment. He had already banged in all seven and was yanking them out so he could start again. He started banging away joyfully but didn't notice the effect it had on Robbie Henry. Robbie was short for his age and had a prominent nose that was just short of a beak. He was cupping his hands over his ears and loudly screaming.

"Stop it!"

Darcy looked up from her gas bill. She put it all away in her desk drawer, crossed over to Robbie, and squatted down so she was face-to-face with him.

"What's wrong, honey?"

"He won't stop! Make him stop!"

"It's just 'me time.' Maybe you need to find something to do."

"It's too loud!" Robbie snapped. "Make him stop."

Justin stopped pounding briefly and looked at Robbie defiantly.

"No way. You can't stop me!"

Robbie launched himself forward, knocking Darcy over. She landed on a pile of cardboard blocks. Robbie pushed a blonde girl out of the way and grabbed Justin.

"Hey, let go!" Justin yelled. But Robbie, eyes wild, bit Justin again and again like a mad dog. Darcy got up and spun around.

"Help, Miss Mellon!" Justin screamed. The girls squealed in terror as Robbie sank his teeth into Justin's leg. Darcy pulled Robbie off of Justin and flung him to her right. Robbie landed on his butt against the wall. Darcy shuddered. She looked over at Robbie, but she had to look twice to be sure she was seeing what she thought she was seeing. Robbie was foaming at the mouth.

Keith Cramper ran out of the classroom, yelling for help. Darcy looked toward her kids and yelled, "All right, everybody in the hallway. Stay away from Robbie. Let's move it, children."

The kids ran out. Darcy carried the crying and wincing Justin. She kept one eye on Robbie. She'd had kids bite before. It was the cost of doing business in preschool. But she'd never had a kid bite another kid multiple times and, as a frightening finale, foam at the mouth. She generally knew each one of her student's medical conditions, and Robbie didn't have a history of epilepsy. She'd seen it on some medical show a few years back, but Robbie, she suspected, had another problem.

Alvin Teeter, the teacher across the hall, came to the door. He carried Justin to the nurse. Darcy tried to approach Robbie, but at every attempt he snapped at her.

"Come on, Robbie. Why don't you calm on down a bit?" But Robbie acted like a trapped animal. Darcy wasn't keen on getting bitten and backed off.

Principal Johnson, a tall, authoritarian African American arrived at the door and asked what had happened. Darcy filled him in, and Johnson looked toward Robbie. He could see Justin's blood was on Robbie's mouth, turning the foam a gruesome pink. Johnson pulled Darcy out of the room and closed the door.

"You get ahold of his parents right quick," Johnson said. "I'm going to call an ambulance and get this boy to the hospital."

The ambulance arrived ten minutes later. The paramedics were used to handling violent patients. They grabbed Robbie, strapped him to a stretcher, and whisked him away. The halls were filled with throngs of panicked students. Principal Johnson tried to keep everyone calm.

Darcy used Principal Johnson's office and tried several times to call the Henry house. At first, no one answered at any of the numbers listed in the card file. Finally, Bert Henry picked up.

"Mr. Henry. This is Darcy Mellon down at Robbie's school. Look, I don't want to alarm you, but he's been taken to the hospital."

"Why?" Bert asked.

"Well, he bit a child numerous times and, well, he had to be removed."

"I'll be right over to the hospital."

When Darcy hung up she found Principal Johnson just outside his office. He was managing the crisis with his natural aplomb. He directed the teachers to move the children into the all-purpose room. He would address them in fifteen minutes. Everyone began to move in that direction.

"Miss Mellon. Did you get a hold of the Henrys?" Principal Johnson asked.

"Yes, sir. Mr. Henry's on his way to the hospital."

"Do me a favor and run on down there and see if you can find out what's wrong with that boy. Never seen anything like it."

"But my class."

"Don't worry about your class. I may cancel classes today. Just get on over there and ascertain what's going on. You're my eyes and ears."

Darcy headed out to the teacher's parking lot and hopped in her new Sentra.

She drove to Texarkana Memorial Hospital and parked. She asked the receptionist where Robbie Henry was but didn't need to wait for the answer. The ER doors swung open, and she could hear Robbie snarling and wailing. Darcy was moving tentatively toward the swinging doors when she noticed

Bert Henry and his wife Martha sitting in the waiting area. The last time Darcy had seen them was at the school's Halloween Monster Mash.

Martha looked pale and tense. She had changed dramatically since the Monster Mash. She was breathing heavily. Darcy approached Bert and offered her hand.

"Mr. Henry."

"Miss Mellon."

"Does the doctor know what's wrong with him? Why he did this?"

Bert stood and pulled Darcy aside around the corner near a coffee cart on wheels. Bert's eyes welled up. Darcy grabbed a napkin off the cart and handed it to him. Bert spoke with a thick and deep Southern drawl. He looked like a simple man whose life had just become far too complicated.

"There's madness on my wife's side of the family. It all seemed to hit at once. I don't know how to deal with this."

"Madness?"

"I had to institutionalize my daughter last week."

"My God."

Martha marched over to them, shoving a passing doctor out of the way. She stood between Bert and Darcy.

"What are you saying to her! Are you talking about me? This is all her fault," Martha said, turning to Darcy. "What did you do to my boy?"

"Ma'am, I can assure you we didn't do anything." Martha's fury grew with every step she took toward Darcy. Darcy had dealt with angry mothers before but not with anything like this. Martha's fists were clenched, and her neck was tightening. "Robbie just kind of went off."

"Who said you could call him Robbie!" Bert tried to calm his wife, as they now had the full attention of everyone on the floor.

"Take it easy, honey."

Martha shoved Bert, and he fell into the coffee cart, sending the large cardboard carriers of Sumatra spilling across the floor. Martha lunged at Darcy and grabbed her neck. Darcy broke free but then slipped on the coffee. Martha pounced and bit Darcy's arm. Darcy yelped in pain and took her foot and put it on Martha's chest. She gave it a reflexive shove and Martha flew backward, nearly knocking over an old man using a walker. Martha jumped to her feet, and Darcy jumped back. Martha was foaming at the mouth just like Robbie had.

Martha charged for Darcy. Martha's unholy scream filled the lobby. Darcy was cornered and didn't have a way to escape. She instinctively covered her face and missed the moment the two massive orderlies grabbed Martha from behind. She kicked and screamed as they dragged her to a gurney and strapped her in.

Bert broke down in tears.

"Oh my God, oh my God." He chanted this over and over, like a prayer.

The orderlies pushed Martha through the ER doors, and Bert ran after her. His whole world was collapsing around him.

The ER doctor Jack Underwood—a lean, narrow-faced man who was sorely in need of a haircut—came up to Darcy and looked at the bite on her arm.

"She bit you?"

"Yes. I was just trying to help."

"Look, I need to you to stick around."

"Oh, just give me a bandage. I should be fine."

"I don't think so, Miss…"

"Mellon. Darcy Mellon. I'm Robbie Henry's teacher."

"Oh, so you saw what happened."

"Yeah, it was a lot like the mother. Husband said there's madness in the family. He tell you that? "

"Yes, but that's not the problem."

"Then what is?"

"Look, I normally wouldn't disclose this, but since you've been bitten, I have no choice."

"Disclose what?"

"Miss Mellon, I think that your student is in advanced-stage rabies exposure."

"Rabies?"

"And by the looks of the mother, she probably is too. I have to do some blood tests to make certain. But if they come back positive, you'll have to start a rabies series immediately."

"How bad is this?" Darcy said as the blood drained from her face.

"Oh, you have nothing to worry about. You just sit tight here, and I'll come out to get you."

Darcy sat down. When she was a kid in the country, her brother Newland got bit by a rabid squirrel and had to go through a long series of painful shots. She hoped that technology had improved since then, but she wasn't counting on it.

She sat there for the better part of an hour. She managed to call Principal Johnson and fill him in. He told Darcy he'd be down to the hospital within the half hour.

Principal Johnson arrived in twenty minutes and rushed to Darcy's side. He was out of breath. He sat next to her and gripped her arm and assured her that she'd be all right.

"This is all my fault."

"No, it isn't."

"I should have come down here. I shouldn't have sent you."

"I'll be okay."

"You find out what's wrong with the boy?"

"Rabies."

Principal Johnson sat there speechless. He asked if it was possible if the school was responsible for the infection. Darcy said she doubted it, as Mrs. Henry was also a victim of the disease.

While Darcy and Principal Johnson waited, an ambulance pulled up. The paramedics wheeled in an unconscious little girl. It was the Henrys' daughter being transferred from the institution that she'd been placed in. Dr. Underwood wanted to do tests on her to find out if she was also a victim.

A pudgy nurse in dark red surgical scrubs approached Darcy.

"You're Darcy Mellon?"

"Yes."

"Dr. Underwood wants to start you on your rabies series."

"So the tests were positive on Mrs. Henry?"

"He wouldn't have ordered them if they weren't."

"Excuse me. Shouldn't the doctor be telling us this? This sounds pretty serious," Principal Johnson said.

"Dr. Underwood has his hands full. He hoped you'd understand."

"Well, I don't. One of my employees has been exposed to a disease on hospital grounds. I find this unacceptable."

"I'll tell the doctor," the pudgy nurse said.

Johnson went with Darcy into the exam room to start her shots.

"You don't have to come," Darcy said.

"I wouldn't be anywhere else."

"Thank you."

Darcy was surprised how much he seemed to care about her welfare. They'd barely exchanged more than four words all year, but obviously he cared about his teachers; that made Darcy feel more secure.

They sat in an exam room, and Dr. Underwood passed by and grabbed a phone that was in the room opposite them. He dialed and put it on speakerphone. Principal Johnson looked at Darcy.

"Is that him?"

"Yes."

"I'm going to have a word."

Principal Johnson started for Underwood, but Darcy held him back. Dr. Underwood had gotten through. A voice came out of the speakerphone as Underwood looked at a stack of charts.

"Dr. Dunn."

"Dr. Dunn, this is Dr. Underwood. I'm down in Texarkana."

"Yes?"

"You had an alert that you had put out. Part of that CDC protocol."

"The families? Yes."

"Well, I think I've got your third family. Rabies. Late stage, I think."

"Are you sure?"

Darcy and Principal Johnson grew quiet and listened.

"I got chem panels back on two of them, and they're positive. I'm testing the father and the daughter, and I'll have the results by around six."

"Can they be transported?"

"I suppose. Where?"

"Here. I need them here. Medevac them."

"I can't sign off on that without…"

"Who's the chief? Margot?"

"Yeah."

"I'll talk to her. Get those patients up here now!"

Dr. Underwood hung up and realized he'd left the door open. He looked toward Darcy coldly and closed it.

As her shots were administered, orderlies ran back and forth. Later, Darcy and Principal Johnson caught sight of the Henry family being taken by gurney out of the hospital.

Darcy would later look out her exam window and see the medevac chopper speeding away with the Henry family on board.

CHAPTER 16

A brilliant morning sun breaking through the window at a perfect angle bathed Dave's face in sunlight. He hadn't slept well. Dave had tossed and turned till around three in the morning. His mind was running, and he couldn't depend on Patrón anymore. Finally, Dave slipped off into a deep sleep. He managed to get in four solid hours before the sun finally woke him.

Dave decided he needed to see if the lab results had shown up yet. He picked up the phone and called Paula's room, but there was no answer. Dave hoped he hadn't overslept and missed some important meeting.

He quickly took a shower, put on his spare suit, and headed down to the dining room. He found Paula eating bacon and eggs. Paula put her fork down and swallowed. Dave sat with her, arching his eyebrows, inspecting her plate.

"I thought that pork wasn't on the Muslim fine-dining list."

"Don't say anything," Paula warned.

"Hey, I can't blame you. Bacon is the perfect food."

"After pepperoni pizza."

"So how's it work? You eat bacon and you throw in an extra prayer?"

"Funny." She sat back patted her tight stomach. "Look, you live in the South, you eat like a Southerner."

"Tell that to Allah."

Dave snared the remaining bacon off her plate and gobbled it down. Paula gave him a dirty look.

"Hey, I'm ensuring your place in heaven. Thank me later."

He stopped a passing waitress.

"I'll have another heart-attack plate like she's having."

"Sure."

The waitress wandered off. Dave noticed a manila folder on the table. Paula wiped her hands with a napkin and slid it over to him.

"Just got this."

Dave opened it, getting bacon grease on it. Paula handed him a napkin. Dave wiped his hands and pulled the sheets of paper out of the envelope.

"Lab results?"

"They worked through the night. Pearson was at my door at seven o'clock."

Dave flipped through the pages, and they indicated a trace of plague and botulism in the area where the booth had been located. Dave sat back and looked at Paula. His eyebrows furrowed.

"Good thing we started our antibiotics last night."

"I know. I spoke to the New York office already. They've gotta close that section of the mall. Who else could have been exposed by now? I mean, thousands of shoppers go through there every day."

"It's in an area that's usually pretty quiet. The chance of infection is pretty unlikely."

"Then why are we taking cipro?"

"'Cause we were nosing around right where it happened. You tell Pearson?"

"Yeah, he was a little upset you didn't write him a prescription."

"I'll call something in."

Dave looked at another sheet of paper that was stuck in the envelope. Dave reviewed it with customary speed.

"What's that?" Paula asked.

"Another potential problem. There's some other substances they haven't identified yet. Great."

"Why not?"

"Because you gotta test for just about every nasty thing you can think of. It takes time. We knew what we were looking for, and that's why we got quick results. But we don't know if there's anything else in the mix."

"Is there anything worse out there?"

"Sure, but we'd be dead by now," Dave said.

"Okay, so we've found the point of infection. But how'd he do it? How'd get the disease into them?"

"I have no idea. Some families walk around a corner and come out with deadly diseases. One you traditionally get from ingesting and another that tends to be airborne. Yet they were exposed at the same time. And the even bigger question is why in the hell would he do it?"

"Look, it smelled like terrorism to me from the get-go, but that guy didn't exactly look like a terrorist."

Dave feigned shock that these words would come out of Paula's mouth. He took her cup of coffee and drank from it. Dave smiled and said.

"Oh, really, Agent Mushari. What do terrorists look like?"

Paula leaned forward and gave him a wry grin.

"Like my cousins Medja and Tali. What do you think?"

"If *I* said that you'd be down my throat."

"That's right. I can say it. You can't."

"You have the cultural advantage on me?"

"Something like that."

Dave laughed and slid the lab report back into the file.

"Any ID on the guy yet?" Dave asked Paula.

"No, they're still searching."

"So what do we do?"

"We wait."

Paula went upstairs. She had a conference call with the New York office on how to handle the mall situation.

Dave's cell phone rang, and he snatched it, nearly dropping it. He didn't bother to see who was calling. He assumed it was Paula with the ID. But another voice was on the other end. It was Dr. Root.

"Hi, Dave. How's it going up there?"

"Well, there's definitely something brewing. Looks like some character infected some people with botulinum and bubonic plague. They're still trying to track him down. How's it going down there?"

There was a long silence. Dr. Root cleared his throat.

"Your review didn't go well. Lussier wants you out at the end of the month," Dr. Root said. "I hate to be blunt, but there's no use in sugar coating it."

"But doesn't he realize what's going on up here?"

"He doesn't care. He thinks it's an FBI issue."

"But I'm in the counterterrorism division of the CDC," Dave said.

"Yeah, and he spoke to the director of the New York office, and he said the suspect seems like a localized homicidal maniac. They doubt there's a terrorism angle, so isn't in your purview."

"Can't you go over his head?" Dave asked.

"Come on, Dave. You know how well that would go over. I can't do that. I've been busting my butt to turn this guy around, but he won't budge."

"Can I stay on this while I still have a job?"

"Look, you got twelve days. Use it however you like. But your voucher is rescinded as of…"

"Rescinded! Where am I supposed to stay?"

"Look, all I can do is keep you on payroll. But I can't cover your hotel. I know it's unreasonable, but he's tied my hands."

"Well, maybe I can turn things around."

"I sincerely hope you do."

Dr. Root hung up. Dave realized he'd never been fired from anything in his life, and now due to his drinking problem, he was out of a job. In twelve days he wouldn't be able to do what he loved to do anymore.

It was a little after eleven thirty in the morning when Dave looked up and noticed Paula Mushari walking into the Holiday Inn. He was seated at the bar. He had a margarita in front of him filled to the top. She watched him for a minute before she approached. He just stared at the drink.

Paula walked over and took the stool next to him. Dave glanced over, and their eyes met. He felt she could see right through him.

"Well, something tells me that you're not supposed to be in here," Paula said. "You've been staring at that drink, and it isn't even lunchtime yet."

"What are you, a detective?"

"Yeah."

Dave sighed heavily and leaned back in his stool. He played with a stirrer in the drink and looked at Paula.

"They sacked me."

"The CDC? Why?"

"Too many cocktails."

"But you're on the wagon. Correct?"

"I have been."

"So let me get this right. Your solution is to bury yourself in that alcohol that got you fired?"

"Exactly."

"You gotta go back tomorrow?"

"I've got just short of two weeks left on the job."

"Then why don't you use them wisely?"

Paula took the margarita and placed it behind the counter. His eyes followed the drink. He looked between Paula and the margarita for a moment. He forced a painful smile. Dave got up from the bar, pushing himself away.

"Thanks, Paula."

"You're lucky I'm Muslim. I'm not supposed to drink."

"You eat bacon."

"I pick and choose my vices."

"They've also killed my voucher."

"So you're homeless?"

"That's the deal."

"Do you snore?" Paula said smiling.

"You want to be roomies?"

"Sure. I'll get you a spare key. We should get outta here."

As they got into the lobby, Dave's cell rang and he answered it. It was Dr. Dunn.

"Dr. Richards, we've checked all the families that were on the church-group trip and they're clean. What we didn't know was that there was a family from Texarkana. They all came down with rabies. I had them transported up here. "

"My God. You sure? What's their condition?"

"Well, can you tell me the infection date?" Dunn said.

"It had to be at least two weeks."

There was a long, drawn-out, shared silence on the phone. Dave knew what that meant and Dunn had to, too.

"I'm sorry," Dave added finally. Paula looked on with confusion.

"Look, we'll try to get back there tonight. See if there's anything I can do." The only remote chance this family had was a skilled toxicologist like himself. Dave hung up and filled Paula in. They packed their bags and headed to JFK.

Their plane got priority clearance and took off ahead of the conga line of jets headed for all parts of the world. Paula sat next to Dave on the flight this time.

"You okay?" Paula asked.

"Been better."

"Look, you've just had a run of bad luck."

"I guess you could call it that."

"You are exceptional at what you do. You know that."

Dave looked into her beautiful eyes and was taken with her kindness and warmth. Lately, that had been in short supply, and it felt good.

"Thanks."

"I don't want to lose you over some office controversy."

"You're going to try to pull some strings?"

"Maybe. I mean, we had the New York office of the FBI jumping through hoops for us. Maybe I can get the CDC to do the same thing."

"You're an optimist."

"Dave, I've found that people do their best work when they are really under the gun."

"Then I guess I'm your man. How are we going to pull this together in twelve days?"

"You don't have a choice. If you don't, the CDC job is gone. If you do, they can't fire you. Look, we make a great team. Let's just keep going."

"Were you a cheerleader in high school?"

"I was on the pep squad, yes. It has helped me in all my endeavors," she said proudly.

"Okay, we'll save the world in twelve days."

"Good. I say we hit the fridge and kick back till we get to Little Rock."

Paula tugged at his arm, and Dave followed her over to the fridge where they surveyed their choices.

CHAPTER 17

Agent Pearson sat at his desk and looked at the picture of the unidentified man from the mall in New York. He picked it up, and a second copy fell out beneath the picture. Pearson had ordered a copy so that it could be used to find a match. He picked up the second picture and walked over to one of the assistants, Tanya, who was typing.

"Tanya."

"Yes."

"Why is this picture still on my desk?"

"You said you wanted a copy."

"I said I wanted a copy, and I wanted it taken down to the eighth floor."

"Oh, I thought you wanted a copy."

"This is important, Tanya. Come on."

"I'm sorry, I'll take it down."

"No, we've lost over twenty-four hours on this."

"Are you going to bring it up to my supervisor?"

"I'm surprised that's all you're worried about."

Pearson grabbed the picture and walked to the elevator. He punched the button, and the car arrived swiftly.

Down on the eighth floor, Pearson looked for the department locations and found the one called Suspect ID. It was on the far end of the floor, and he had to walk through a labyrinth of halls. He reached a room that was managed by a young man wearing thick, coke-bottle glasses. He shook Pearson's hand.

"Hi, I'm Stewart. How can I help you?"

"I'm Agent Pearson. I got this character here. No ID. We need you to put him at the head of the pile."

"I got about twenty other guys that are at the head of the pile."

"I don't care. I need this now."

"This is a pretty involved process. The computer has to try and find a match." Stewart looked at the picture and frowned.

"And the image quality is low. I could get ten matchups, easy."

"Then you better get started," Pearson said firmly.

"Okay, all right. What's your extension?"

"Three-seven-two-seven."

Stewart wrote down the number on the picture. Pearson headed out of the Suspect ID office shaking his head. He looked back toward Stewart, who had taken a call that seemed to be of a casual nature.

Pearson couldn't help but think that they were asleep at the switch and if they weren't careful it could all come back and reflect negatively on the FBI. He knew that something was brewing with this case. He could feel it. He just needed to get the worker bees to pay attention.

He got back on the elevator and punched the button for the tenth floor. Pearson remembered that's where Tanya's supervisor was, and he wanted to have a few words with her.

CHAPTER 18

The FBI jet touched down at Little Rock and taxied to the northern end of the modest airport. Dave Richards opened the door and headed down the steps, followed by Paula. A pair of state police cars raced up to them and stopped. A tall state trooper hopped out of his car and ran up to the pair.

"Dr. Richards. Agent Mushari?"

"Yes." Dave shook the trooper's hand.

"Dr. Dunn needs you immediately at the hospital."

Dave and Paula were put in one of the state patrol cars. The trooper rapped the roof of the car, and the driver sped out, sirens blazing. Dave and Paula barely said a word as they headed down the highway at over ninety miles an hour.

When they reached the hospital, Dr. Dunn was waiting at the entrance.

"How are the Munsens?" Dave asked.

"Stable, making great progress. Still unconscious," Dr. Dunn said.

"The Kelloggs?"

"Mother was touch and go. I adjusted the medications, and I think we're out of the woods. But I'm keeping them heavily sedated."

Dave strode into the hospital and looked back at Dr. Dunn.

"What about the Henrys?"

Dr. Dunn took off his glasses and rubbed his eyes. Dave noticed that Dunn looked tired and scared.

"I'm afraid that this has gone beyond my expertise," Dunn said, putting his glasses back on. Dave faced Dr. Dunn.

"This isn't really about expertise, Dr. Dunn. Your patients could be at the point of no return. I'm going to do my best but…well…let's see the patients."

Dr. Dunn nodded and brought them up to the Henrys' floor. Paula followed closely behind Dave and Dr. Dunn. She listened in on their conversation, but they might as well have been speaking in Latin. Doctors spoke in their own language and rarely translated.

Dave looked sadly at the Henry family. Several nurses stood by, hoping to follow instructions that could save the Henrys. Dave reviewed the charts and had a whispered conversation with Dr. Dunn. Dave nodded as he tried to see how they should proceed. Dr. Dunn stepped away to answer a call, and Paula moved up to Dave.

"How are they doing?" Paula asked.

"Mother and daughter are both in a coma."

"Oh. Not good."

"No, this is what rabies does."

The device monitoring Robbie's vitals started to beep rapidly, indicating tachycardia. The nurses raced over to attend, but Dave didn't move. Paula looked at him, surprised.

"Aren't you going to do anything?" Paula said.

"You ever had a dog bite?"

"When I was a kid."

"See, if the dog was suspected as being rabid, your doctor would start a post-exposure prophylaxis."

"What's that?"

"It's a course of treatment that requires a series of shots."

"Yeah, well why don't you do that?"

Dave gently tugged Paula away from the nurses working on Robbie. He closed the sliding door and sat down on a chair in the hallway. Paula sat next to him. Dave looked grim.

"I can't do that because they are well past the incubation period. If they were exposed to the rabies virus more than two weeks ago, the mortality rate is one hundred percent."

"Rabies? Nobody dies from rabies."

"Not in this country, not anymore. But in India it's in the tens of thousands."

"You mean to tell me that whole family's going to die?"

"I'm afraid so."

Paula sat back, shaking her head.

"Why would anyone do this?"

"And how? First we have botulism, which is ingested; then plague, which is breathed in or comes from flea bites; and finally rabies, which comes from animal bites. Somehow he infected all these people. Can't find out from the patients what happened. They're either dying or unconscious."

Dave stood up and looked in the window at the Henrys. Then he walked down the hall to where the Munsens were recovering. Paula followed him. Dave looked back toward the Henrys.

"My God," Dave said.

"What?"

"He's running a series."

"Series of what?"

"Series of tests. Uh, terrorists groups often do dry runs to find out what's the most effective method of, well, killing."

"So the guy is planning something bigger?"

"It's the only thing that makes sense. Okay, let's say you're a homicidal maniac, and you want to kill someone. You pick your poison."

"You'd choose one toxin, not three."

"Exactly. This guy has a plan, and the families in here are his test subjects."

Paula grabbed Dave and pulled him into an unoccupied intake room. Dave looked at her, puzzled.

"What are you doing?"

"If you're right then there is someone monitoring the data results."

"Right, of course. If you're doing a proper study someone would have to…"

Paula looked at him, and he turned and gazed out the small window of the intake room.

"This is nuts," Dave said.

"Nope, we're doing great. I told you we made a good team." At this point Dave was just playing theorist and armchair detective. He turned back to Paula.

"We've got to assume that there's someone doing…on-site data collection."

Paula reflexively checked her gun and opened the door of the intake room. She surveyed the varied faces, and no one struck her as out of place.

An alarm went off, and someone loudly called a code. Robbie Henry's heart had stopped, and the staff were working feverishly to save him. Dr. Dunn came running down to assist, but Robbie's time of death was called a half hour later. The entire Henry family would die over the next twenty-four hours.

CHAPTER 19

Tunis Ganji was a Pakistani national and had been in the United States for two years. Tunis had felt comfortable in New York, but he didn't care for Little Rock. He stood out like a sore thumb. He was dark skinned but clearly not black. His accent was thick, and the locals always whispered behind his back. He was lonely. He couldn't get close to anyone because he had a specific assignment to carry out.

As intake coordinator at the hospital, it was his job to obtain insurance approval for each patient. His demeanor was cold, and that suited the department head well.

At lunchtime the hospital floor was often empty. There was a barbecue restaurant called Q's that the nurses favored across the street. Tunis always brought his lunch so he'd have an excuse not to go out.

As the nurses made their way to Q's, Tunis went to the Henrys' room, pulled out a small scanner he kept in his briefcase, and copied the charts at the end of their beds.

Tunis would swiftly gather the information and transmit it by plugging the scanner into his cell phone and sending it to New York, where Oren would retrieve the data and review it.

They had thorough files that began with the forms the families had filled out at the mall in New York.

When the Henrys died, Tunis collected the data off their charts for the final time. He went down to the basement of the hospital and sent the data to New York. Tunis was glad it was over. It meant he could get out of Arkansas. He couldn't stand the people or the food. New York was more like home. There were restaurants that made his favorite dishes, and he could occasionally play a chess game in the park with some Pakistanis he'd befriended. Tunis thought the operation had gone perfectly until he saw Paula Mushari come out of the elevator flashing her FBI badge. Paula hadn't seen him, but he knew why she was there. When he saw her join Dr. Dunn, he was certain the FBI was already investigating the deaths.

Tunis took the stairs and quietly walked out of the hospital. He got in his car and drove into Little Rock. He had to be careful. He had to get word out that the cell's plans might be compromised.

He parked near an upscale plaza and walked to a Verizon store. He bought a disposable phone and endured the curious and suspicious looks from the salesmen. Tunis found a desolate alley and called Oren. Oren answered.

"Yes."

"It's Tunis. We have a problem."

"What are you talking about? The test went perfectly."

"You don't understand. I saw an agent talking to the doctor in charge. I'm telling you, they are suspicious."

Oren was silent on the other end of the phone.

"Who is? F, C, or D?" F was for FBI, C was for CIA, and D was for the Defense Intelligence Agency.

"F," Tunis responded.

"What do they know?"

"I don't know. You said that no one would pay attention to this phase in a small town. How could this happen? Maybe this was all a mistake."

"Stop panicking."

"You weren't fifty feet away from a fed. I was."

"Be careful what you say."

"I'm sorry."

Oren looked down at his feet, pondering his next move. They were close to putting their plan into action, and they couldn't pull the plug now. There was only one thing to do, and he knew what it was.

"You must stop them."

"Stop them?" Tunis said nervously as a passerby looked down the alley.

"Yes. Stop them. Do you understand?" Oren said.

"Do you want me to try to throw them off?"

"I suggest termination," he said with finality.

"Termination?" Tunis took this in. It's what he had signed up for, and now he had to do the same kind of dirty work that Ben had to do to prove his loyalty.

Tunis was silent, and he took in a deep breath.

"Do you understand?" Oren repeated.

"I will tend to the problem."

Tunis closed his cell phone and walked out of the alley. He crossed a bridge and tossed the phone into a river that ran beneath it. Tunis got back into his car. He sighed heavily and checked for his gun in the glove compartment. He thought he'd never have to use it.

CHAPTER 20

Agent Moltidani was glad to be back in New York. He had spent the last four months in Idaho working on the Knights of the White Order case and looked forward to visiting his family in the Bronx. But the first thing he had to do before rejoining his family was to stop by and see Frank Gilmore. Frank was getting married, and Moltidani was the best man.

Moltidani met Frank on the twentieth floor, and they embraced and carried on loudly. Frank was from the Bronx, too, but usually had to be reserved like the other agents. Frank looked around and noticed all eyes were on them. Frank told Moltidani to quiet down.

"How can you stand this? Bunch a stiffs around here," Moltidani complained.

"Yeah, but I get to wear a suit, and that attracts a better class of lady."

"Really? Who'd you con into marrying you?"

"Okay, used to be a model. Has a law degree. Got a job on Wall Street."

"She rich or something?"

"Richer than me."

"Seriously. You're marrying a chick who's richer than you?"

"Absolutely."

"Okay, but do you like her, Frankie?"

"I love her. All that other stuff is fringe benefits."

A senior agent came out of his office and signaled Frank to come into a meeting that was going on.

"Hang out. I'll be right back," Frank said.

Moltidani paced the floor, then finally landed in a seat behind a desk in the bullpen. He looked across it and peered in the inbox and saw an upside-down picture that looked familiar. He turned it around and realized it was a picture of Ben Curran.

"Can I help you?" Agent Pearson approached the desk.

"Uh, sorry. I was just waiting for Gilmore."

"You're in my chair."

"Sorry, I was just wondering what you were doing with that picture."

"Trying to identify him. Part of a big case up here."

"You don't know who he is?"

"No, I'm still waiting to get a hit on him."

"Is he in New York?"

"I don't give out information on investigations to total strangers."

"Well, I'm about to become the best friend you've ever had. I know who this guy is. I almost caught him in Idaho. You better get your boss down here."

CHAPTER 21

Kathy Dunbar's office was larger than some of the doctors'. She was the head of hospital personnel, and her ego matched the size of her office. She was a prim woman with a slight build. Not one hair was out of place as it was neatly tied in a bun. She still wore a wedding ring, although she'd been divorced for three years.

The idea that she may have hired a terrorist was inconceivable. Kathy rarely made mistakes, and she did thorough background checks on all her employees.

It only took a brief time to narrow down the possibilities. Only one name stood out. Omar Kapur—this was the name that Khalid had created for Tunis.

"Where is Omar?" Paula asked.

"Well, I assume he's in intake where he belongs," Kathy said arrogantly.

Paula rose. "We better go talk to him."

Kathy stood and headed down the hall with Dave and Paula close on her heels. Kathy came to the intake room where several patients were sitting across from employees who were inputting their data into computers.

"Excuse me," Kathy said. "Where's Omar?" One of the intake girls piped up.

"He took an early lunch an hour ago. Kind of weird 'cause he always eats in." Kathy looked at Dave and Paula.

"This can't be happening. We're very thorough," Kathy said, holding back her growing panic.

"So are they," Dave said. "He probably saw us and took off."

Paula told Kathy to compile any information about Omar and give it to the Arkansas state police. Kathy nodded and quickly rushed back to her office. Paula started dialing the state police, but her cell phone rang. She answered it.

"Agent Mushari."

"It's Pearson."

"Agent Pearson, what's going on?"

"We ID'd your guy. Ben Curran. Twenty-six years old. Member of the Knights of the White Order. ATF's been on him for a couple months."

"A white supremacist?"

"Yeah, remember Harlan Curran? It's his son."

Paula did remember. She had followed the Idaho case in the papers. There had been alerts that Ben might make his way into Arkansas, but she hadn't been officially part of that briefing.

"Look, Dr. Richards thinks these sick families here are test cases. And we think we've got a connection to a Pakistani national called Omar Kapur. Doubt that's his real name, but it looks like they may be connected."

There was a long silence on the other end of the phone. Pearson cleared his throat.

"How is he connected?"

"It's only supposition, but we think he was collecting the data on the patients."

"You better get back here ASAP."

Paula hung up and started out of the hospital. Dave followed closely behind her. They stepped out of the ER door into the cool of late autumn. Dave tugged at Paula's jacket.

"Okay, so what was that about?"

"Terrorists have a hard time moving around because they set off alarm bells. Sleeper cells are independent, but they have American eyes on them. Our guy is a white supremacist who's working with an Arab terror cell."

"A white sleeper?"

"Exactly. We've been afraid of this for a long time."

Paula had called ahead and had her car brought from the airport. It was a black Honda coupe with silver trim. Dave got into the passenger seat.

"Where are we going?"

"They took our bags to my office. We'll go get them and get back on the jet."

Paula pulled out of the hospital parking lot and headed down a country road. Paula had become very familiar with the area while assigned here, so she chose the quickest route to the airport, even though the road through the farmlands was narrow and rather isolated.

"How would they recruit a guy like Curran for their cause?" Dave said.

"Money, I guess."

"But aren't they the last people he'd want to be in business with?"

While Paula pondered this, she didn't notice Tunis pull up behind them in his Ford Explorer.

Tunis had his gun lying on the seat next to him and rolled down the window. Tunis hadn't fired a gun since terrorist training camp at the Pakistani-Afghan border three years ago. Tunis put his gun in his left hand, which was difficult since he was right handed. He wanted to pull up next to her Honda, but it was a small, two-lane road, and there was too much oncoming traffic. He aimed at Paula's car while they zoomed along the lonely, two-lane highway. He squeezed the trigger and fired.

The bullet punctured the rear window, and Paula swerved. Dave looked in the mirror and saw the Arab. He ducked. The bullet missed him by inches and became embedded in the glove compartment.

"It's him."

"Yeah, I figured."

She sped up and swerved in front of a pickup truck. Another shot rang out, skipping across the roof. Paula looked at Dave, who was tucked in the corner of the passenger side.

"You look like you've never been shot at."

"I'm a doctor. I get sued, not shot at."

Paula snapped the wheel right and hit the brakes. Tunis raced in front of her, and Paula pulled in behind Tunis. Dave sat up.

"How'd you do that?"

Paula looked at Dave, a little surprised.

"It's part of our training."

The two vehicles sparred down the highway. Dave was in awe of Paula's skill behind the wheel, and she wasn't even breaking a sweat.

Tunis tried to shoot behind him, but it was useless. Paula faked right, then left. Tunis hit the gas and sped up to a little under ninety, and Paula stayed right on him.

Paula gunned the engine and came up alongside him, hit the brakes, and slid to the other side. Tunis yanked the wheel right but turned too sharply. The tires squealed for a brief moment. Then the Explorer turned sideways and flipped end over end. Glass flew in every direction as the vehicle rolled off the road, down an embankment, and into a rushing river.

Paula and Dave came to halt on the side of the road. They sprinted toward the Explorer, which was already half covered in water. Dave was ahead of Paula and leapt to the car that was lying on its side.

"Careful!" Paula yelled.

Dave looked into the car. The window was broken, and he could see Tunis, still in the driver's seat underneath two feet of water. Dave reached in and tried to release Tunis's seat belt but couldn't get a good hold on it. The water from the river was relentless. It had busted through the back window, and the car was filling up fast.

Paula watched the power of the river push the Explorer several yards and nearly tip the car over.

"Dave, get out of there!" Paula shouted.

Dave couldn't hear her over the rushing water. He reached in again, got a hold of the seat belt, and managed to release it. He grabbed Tunis's collar and pulled him out of the SUV. Dave looked down and saw that the bank of the river was getting farther away—he only had one chance. He threw Tunis over his shoulder, squatted, and thrust out, sending himself and Tunis onto the very edge of the riverbank. Water rushed over them, but Paula helped them get onto solid ground.

As soon as Paula pulled them toward shore, the river slammed into the Explorer and took it downriver where it disappeared. Dave jumped into action in an attempt to save Tunis's life. He did a series of chest compressions and tried mouth to mouth. He repeated this for the next two minutes until there was blood coming out of Tunis's mouth. Tunis had no pulse and was not breathing.

"He's gone?"

"Yeah," Dave said, taking a last look at Tunis. Paula put her hand on his upper back. Dave was breathing hard, almost hyperventilating.

"I did what I could," he said.

"More than some would have done."

"I'm a doctor. That's what we do. Save lives."

"Well, I think we're on the right track," Paula said, helping Dave up to his feet. "You okay?"

"Terrorist tried to kill me, and I tried to save his life, risking mine. I've been better, frankly."

"Somebody told him to do this."

"Well, it's a sure bet it wasn't a case of road rage," Dave said while trying to wring out his clothes.

Dave leaned against a tree and tried to catch his breath. Paula came around to face him. She put one hand on his shoulder and looked into his eyes with concern.

"I'm a toxicologist, Paula. I'm not…you."

"Hey, I wasn't the one pulling the guy out of a car in a river."

"I'm not a hero type."

"Who is? Dave, you're the one who's put this together."

"Yeah, in an office somewhere. You're used to being shot at."

Paula smiled confidently.

"Look, Dr. Richards. " Dave looked at her. She rarely called him that, and it drew his attention. "This is your specialty. We've got some kind of bioterror threat, and you're in the middle of it."

Dave sighed and sat beneath the tree.

"I've been canned, Paula."

"I know. Show them how wrong they were."

Paula sat next to him. Dave looked at her and let his breathing slow down.

"Look, Paula, there are some people in life that are destined for success and some that are destined for failure, and nothing can change that."

"You make your own destiny, Dr. Richards."

Dave considered her words but still felt overwhelmed. His tenure with the CDC was rapidly coming to a close, and uneasy thoughts of alcohol-laced nights had returned. The confrontation with Tunis had awakened the desire for Patrón. But he could suppress it. That was the extent of his control at the moment. He could refuse to pick up the first drink.

Dave listened as Paula called in for an ambulance to pick up Tunis's body. Within twenty minutes the riverbank was crawling with state troopers. The scuba team was called in to recover the Explorer to see what kind of fresh information they could glean from it.

After the incident was related to the New York office, Dave and Paula were summoned back to Manhattan. They found themselves flying back to New York on the FBI jet. It was becoming a home away from home.

When they arrived at JFK, Agent Pearson was not the only one there this time; Director Estes Russell was also in attendance. Russell was a man of average height with green eyes and goat-like eyebrows. He had a disingenuous smile that had probably catapulted him to his current station in life. He slid his arm around Paula, who tried not to shrink from him.

Dave and Paula were treated like chiefs of state on a visit. They were ushered to a fleet of black SUVs that were lined up at the curb. They shared glances with one another, realizing that they were involved in something bigger than they could have possibly imagined.

Director Russell insisted they ride with him. They eased into the black Suburban. When the door closed, the sound of the jets on the tarmac was eliminated.

The SUV began to move swiftly. Agent Pearson was sitting next to Director Russell, who indicated that Pearson give Dave and Paula a pair of files.

"Now, Dr. Richards, what you have there are some thoughts we had on the White Sleeper task force."

"White Sleeper task force?" Dave said, taken aback.

"The director in Washington is calling it that." Russell winked at them.

The director of the FBI was in the loop on this, and that, of course, meant that he actually knew Paula's name. She did her best not to hyperventilate.

"So what's our next move?" Dave asked.

"We need to find this little prick, Curran, and his friends. You've got to move fast 'cause this thing feels like it's bubbling to the top," Russell said.

The phone rang, and Pearson answered it. He whispered to Russell, who nodded. Pearson handed the phone to Dave.

"It's for you," Pearson said. Dave looked at the phone, puzzled.

"Who is it?" Dave asked.

"Channing Zumwalt."

"Who?"

"The president's national security advisor. He'd just like to hear what the implications are of these diseases. Like to hear it from the horse's mouth," Russell said.

Dave said hello and began filling in the national security advisor on the grimy details about plague, rabies, and botulism. Dave handled all the questions with skill and hung up wondering to himself how he'd gone from a basement office in the CDC to talking to a man who was one phone call away from the president. Dave wasn't sure if this was what it meant to make one's own destiny. Until now, he'd been certain he'd squandered his chances. But being suddenly thrown into the middle of this crisis had made him reconsider his dire, albeit cynical, life forecast.

Dave and Paula were dropped off at the Hilton, and Paula checked in. Paula returned to him with a key.

"Come on, roomie."

They headed up to the room and found two beds side by side. Dave chose one while Paula showered and came out wearing a wife beater and some pink boxers. She smelled nice, he thought.

He hadn't lived with a woman in a long time, and he'd forgotten the pleasant smells of shampoos and subtle perfumes.

"You need the TV on to sleep?" she asked.

"Wouldn't hurt."

Paula grabbed the remote and turned on CNN. She hopped in bed.

"'Night."

Paula went to sleep, but Dave had a hard time nodding off. He kept changing positions and ended up with Paula in his line of vision. In the quiet of the night when they weren't involved in the crisis, he noticed how beautiful she was. It kept him up most of the night.

CHAPTER 22

Ben Curran rode the express train to Stamford, Connecticut, at around four in the afternoon. It was just before rush hour, so there weren't many friendly, chatty commuters. The train was fast but had a slight rock to it that almost put him to sleep twice. He would feel like a fool if he missed his stop, so he made several trips up to the snack car to get coffee and something sweet to keep up his energy.

Ben sat back down in his seat as the Connecticut countryside whizzed past him. He dug around in his jacket, searching for the spy novel he'd been working on for the last two weeks. He found it, opened it, and settled in to read.

The book was by a former spy for the KGB. Ben thought he might pick up a few tips. The book proved to be not only entertaining, but also informative. Ben learned about techniques of deception and disinformation. Ben came to respect and revere the protagonist Yuri Polatkin. Ben didn't have heroes, but Yuri was about as close as he was going to get to one.

Ben didn't consider himself a spy per se, but he was living an undercover life; Yuri's words seemed to offer both help and encouragement. The truth was that Ben's plans were being financed by interests in the Middle East. He wasn't aware of who they were, but he knew that when he needed money, it showed up. It could have been Al Qaeda, it could have been Hamas— he didn't know and didn't really care. He was able to do his work the way he wanted it done. The Arabs showed him respect, and he reveled in it.

Oren at first presented him with several half-baked plans to strike the United States, but Ben quickly realized that the Arabs didn't have a clue how to truly strike fear into American hearts. Oren resisted Ben's ideas at first, but soon Ben converted him to Ben's way of thinking. The terrorists agreed to his plan. Ben was feeling good. The ATF raid at the airport had actually turned in his favor. It forced him east and into the path of his new Arab collaborators. Even though Ben privately looked down at them, he marveled at their organization. His buddies of the Knights of the White Order were not the sharpest tools in the shed. But Oren's cell was capable. When Ben asked them to do something, it was done to perfection.

The train began to slow, and the conductor announced Stamford. Ben closed his spy novel and shoved it into his jacket. He stood up and rocked left and right with the train as it slowed and came to a stop.

When Ben stepped down from the train, he took one look and decided that Stamford was the blandest place he'd ever seen. It had no character. He couldn't imagine living in such a neutral place. But obviously many people did. It took him a while to remember why the name Stamford was in the back of his mind, but it finally came to him as he crossed toward a taxi stand.

He was fourteen and had gotten his first wallet condom. His friend Freddie had told him he needed to be prepared at all times. If Ben was going to get laid, he had to be ready on a minute's notice. Ben heeded his advice and managed to get a Trojan from a gas-station vending machine. He never got to use it, but occasionally he'd take it out and read the tiny directions on the back. That's how he noticed that the condom was manufactured in Stamford, Connecticut. Ben thought better of Stamford then.

Ben took a quiet cab ride to a nondescript industrial park. It was a cluster of ten buildings ringed by woods. Autumn was over, and the leaves had blown off the trees. The starkness didn't sit well with Ben. He paid the cab driver, took his card, and said he'd call when it was time to pick him up.

Ben had a short wait in the lobby. A video played in a continuous loop, extolling the great strides of their company. It was a corporate ego trip that probably made the CEO feel like a good guy. Ben went back to his novel; he was reading when a woman came out of a door and headed straight for Ben.

"I'm Cindy Sellars. You must be Ben Jones?"

"That's right."

Later that afternoon Ben Curran dialed a number on his cell phone.

Oren answered. He had been awaiting Ben's call. They had to be cryptic on the phone. The NSA listened to everything out there, so they had to resort to spy speak. The NSA listening devices were programmed to grab words out of the air. If you said the word Al Qaeda, you were flagged. If you said the word Tehran or Bagdad, you were flagged. Most times it led to nothing, but they were thorough; you couldn't make a mistake. You couldn't speak explicitly about blowing up planes or buildings. The NSA computers were so fast and efficient you could find a black ops team on your doorstep. Before you knew it, you'd find yourself in a prison somewhere in Eastern Europe, run by another subset of black baggers.

"I've started my new career," Ben said brightly.

"Ah, good. How are the benefits?" Oren queried.

"As we expected."

"I'm happy for you."

"Great. I'll talk to you later."

Ben hung up.

CHAPTER 23

Ben had learned that the art of not being followed is neither complicated nor daunting. It required simplicity and, more importantly, a place to provide opportunity. The suggested locale to shake off an unwanted tail was the subway system. It offered numerous levels and trains to switch to and passengers to hide behind. This advice came straight from the slim spy novel that Ben Curran had been reading.

Ben left Stamford on the noon train and found himself in Penn Station a little before two.

He made his way to the subway and began his journey to nowhere. He hopped on a train headed uptown for seven stops, crossed over to the other side, and went downtown five stops. He got a cross-town train and waited till the last minute before the doors were about to close, then slipped out. He spent another forty minutes slipping between trains until he was fully satisfied that no one was following him.

When Ben came trotting out of the subway, he was sure that if anyone had his hooks in him, he'd lost him several transfers ago. Ben hadn't been back to the city for a week or so. He had set up a meager life in Stamford.

All seemed to be going well, but Ben didn't like the rapidly increasing communication between him and Oren. He didn't want them to be flagged, so he insisted that the next meeting be face-to-face. He didn't feel he could have a clear conversation in spy speak. They chose a Starbucks near West Fifty-seventh. Ben was running late.

He slipped into the Starbucks and saw that Oren was already seated, sipping a coffee. Ben managed a smile. He was hungry and ordered a coffee and a blueberry muffin. He'd had a taste for blueberry muffins since he had killed the Arab who was eating one. It was strange that after committing a heinous act he became attracted to something so random. Ben felt it had some psychological significance, but it wasn't exactly something you'd go to a shrink about. Ben just resigned himself to a hankering for blueberry muffins.

Ben grabbed his coffee, slid into his seat opposite Oren, and looked around to make sure there was no one near.

"How's the job?"

"Just like you'd imagine. Do you have the data?"

Oren pulled a few sheets of paper out of his jacket pocket and laid it out.

"Tunis was thorough."

"Yeah, I can see that," said Ben.

"They survived the plague? Surprising."

"Botulism too. It wasn't very effective."

Oren turned to the last page, and Ben looked through the notes and smiled. He sipped his coffee and took a big bite out of his blueberry muffin.

"Rabies."

"They all died, Ben. This is a beautiful thing. Once it's in the bloodstream and passes its incubation period, there's nothing they can do."

"But what could a doctor do in Hope?"

"They brought in a specialist, and they still died. I think it's perfect."

"Then it's rabies."

"I agree. There is another issue."

"Issue?"

"Tunis is dead."

"What? How?"

"He was trying to tend to a complication."

"What kind of complication?"

"The FBI stumbled across our test phase."

"How?" Ben was surprised.

"We don't know. But I told Tunis to manage the problem, and then I found out he had died in a car crash."

Ben stood up and indicated he would follow Oren out of the store. Oren got up, leaving his coffee, and walked out to the sidewalk.

"I need the rabies vials now!"

"I have to go through channels."

"I don't care, Oren. We have to move faster, or this could be giant waste of time."

"All right. Relax, Ben. Let me see, I think that I can get it here by tomorrow."

"I'll meet you at the apartment at noon."

"At noon."

"Now stop walking with me."

Oren stopped on the sidewalk as Ben continued his brisk pace into the thick throngs of New Yorkers.

CHAPTER 24

Oren made his way uptown in a cab and was let off a few blocks before his stop. He walked down a grimy alley that was littered with unidentifiable trash. He turned down a dank street and walked past a thickly venting steam grate.

Oren quickened his pace, found a mailbox store, and stepped inside.

The mailbox store was around fifty years old and was lined with bronze mailboxes of all shapes and sizes. Behind the counter was Farid. He was Oren's age, and he looked at him with utter surprise. Farid was Oren's handler, and they were never to meet unless it was under extreme circumstances.

"Farid."

"What are you doing here? Have you been compromised?"

"No. I need a rush job."

Farid came out from behind the counter and crossed to the front door. He put up the closed sign and they disappeared into his rathole of an office in the back. Farid cleared a chair of USPS boxes, and Oren sat down.

"What is it? Quickly!" Farid demanded.

"I need the rabies package by tonight. Tomorrow morning at the latest."

"I thought we had more time."

"We don't."

They spoke in Arabic for another ten minutes and made arrangements. Farid assured Oren that he could deliver it in the time frame. They set a time and place to meet: six a.m. in Central Park.

Oren lit up a cigarette on the way out of the mailbox store. It was one of his last Turkish cigarettes, but he'd accomplished a lot in the last few weeks and decided he deserved one.

CHAPTER 25

Dave ran through the events since he first arrived in Little Rock and wondered, in that phase between sleep and wakefulness, if he'd been right. Was this all his imagination? Dave felt the scrape on his arm that he'd gotten from trying to save the Arab from the submerged Explorer. He sat up in bed and shook off any notion that he had somehow been wrong. He was right. It smelled like a terrorist field test. Now he was a key member of the White Sleeper task force.

He picked up the phone to call Dr. Root and stopped. If he reported to the CDC, he could get pulled from the assignment. Dr. Lussier would likely replace him. Dave didn't owe Lussier anything; Lussier had fired him. If Dave ever wanted to work again, he would need some influential friends. If he helped resolve this crisis, his career might survive this setback.

Dave put the phone back on the cradle. He got dressed and put on his black shirt and slacks. He had to go to the first task-force meeting, and he wanted to look impressive. This was an assumption on his part. He always thought that men who dressed all in black were somehow intimidating. They somehow were trying to be distant and cold in their choice of dress. He was neither distant nor cold, but he felt he needed a mask while dealing with the task-force members.

There was a knock at the door while Dave was tying his tie. He answered it, and Paula was standing there with two cups of coffee.

"Latte?"

"Thanks." He put the coffee down and went back to tying his tie.

"You get any sleep?" she said.

"No. And I need to. This isn't the time to bungle things because I need to take a nap."

Dave fumbled with his tie and started over again.

"It's a huge case. Careers are made on ones like this," Paula said.

"Yeah, but at the expense of the Henry family."

"I didn't mean it that way. We've got a chance to stop the terrorists and keep them from killing more families."

Dave adjusted his tie. He picked up his coffee and took a swig. It went down smoothly. Paula looked at Dave's tie.

"What?"

"You are tired," she said. Paula undid it and began redoing it for him. Paula was very close. Paula finished the tie and patted him on the chest with her palm, and she looked and realized how close they were. She smiled awkwardly and took two steps back from him.

"Much better," she said, turning away.

"Thanks."

Dave sat on the edge of the bed, and Paula sat next to him. Dave looked at her.

"But what if we aren't in time? What if we foul up? We've got to find one guy in a city of nine million people. How do we do that?"

"We don't do it sitting on our asses."

Dave rose from the bed, and Paula followed. They headed down to the lobby where they were met by a waiting car.

Dave and Paula arrived at the FBI building at ten. It was a stark, cold place. The lobby was concrete and dark glass. The reception desk was a dark mahogany that seemed to give off the feel of a stodgy financial institution rather that a law enforcement agency.

They took the elevator up to the tenth floor. As Dave got off, he noted a flyer on the wall warning employees that football pools are considered gambling and wouldn't be tolerated.

Agent Pearson greeted them and shook their hands.

"Agent Mushari, Dr. Richards, we're set up for the meeting in the conference room."

Dave, Paula, and Pearson entered the large conference room. Director Russell sat at the head of the table. Dave recognized the New York City chief of police from seeing him on the news. He was wearing his blue uniform, and his cap rested on the table beside his cell phone.

Each seat had a gray legal pad and pencil laid out. Dave considered taking some water from one of the silver pitchers on the table but thought better of it. He was so nervous, he'd probably spill it.

The seats were all taken, but there were no introductions. Dave assumed that some of the people in the room didn't want to be introduced. This was a domestic case that was under the full supervision of the FBI. But he assumed the CIA would show up…unofficially.

There was a bald man sitting two seats to the right of Director Russell. The bald man nodded to the director. Russell forced an uncomfortable smile. Dave noticed the bald man didn't kowtow to him like the other FBI agents, and Dave suspected, perhaps fancifully, that he was a CIA spook. The man had cold, unfeeling eyes, and Dave could imagine that he managed a cadre of hit men and suffered no remorse. It all seemed a boyish fantasy until Director Russell referred to him as Mr. Smith. Dave was sitting next to Paula and whispered to her.

"Is that bald guy CIA?"

Paula looked to Dave with wide-eyed false innocence.

"What bald guy?"

"The one over there…"

Paula gave Dave an incredulous look. Dave read her eyes and realized that his boyish fantasy was quite probably true. Dave felt self-conscious, and he sat back in his seat and listened intently to Agent Pearson's Power Point presentation on Ben Curran. It reviewed everything that they knew. It was around then that Director Russell looked at Dave.

"Dr. Richards."

Dave looked up, surprised, and started to stand. Paula pulled him back down in his seat.

"Yes sir?"

"These biological weapons. These three. How effective are they?"

"Well, the botulism clearly would not be my weapon of choice. The plague is effective to a degree, but let's face it—a small town doctor beat back the disease, and the patients survived."

"So you are unimpressed by them," Mr. Smith said, coldly pondering something at the end of his long fingers. He dried his hands with a clean white handkerchief and tucked it back into his gray suit.

"That'd be fair to say," Dave said.

"But the rabies killed the Henry family. Correct?" Director Russell asked.

"Yes. After the full incubation period there is 100 percent mortality."

Director Russell stood and walked around the table in a theatric move.

"So you'd bet your money that rabies is the weapon of choice."

"I'd have to, Mr. Director."

"This is absurd," Mr. Smith snarled. "Rabies? Al Qaeda is going to break the back of the United States of America with a disease passed around by biting mammals?" Smith wiped his hands again, quickly dabbing them with his handkerchief.

"In India over fifty thousand people a year die from rabies," Dave said.

"With a population of eight hundred million, the government of India considers that a gift," Mr. Smith slyly chortled.

"Charming sentiment," Dave said before he could check himself. "Look, my point is that if you used it as a bioweapon in this country and people weren't aware they were being infected, the deaths could be far higher than fifty thousand."

Mr. Smith became quiet. Dave thought he better not get on the wrong side of a guy who probably could blow him up in his car. Paula gently patted Dave's thigh under the table, presumably to calm him.

"What kind of delivery system would be used?" a voice at the other end of the table asked.

Dave hadn't fully considered this. He was a toxicologist. He wasn't a bioweapons expert.

"It's unclear."

"Maybe they'll put it in Ken-L Ration," a woman quipped at the end of the table.

The room filled with laughter, and Dave sank in his chair. Director Russell quieted the room.

"Now take it easy, ladies and gentlemen. Dr. Richards is a toxicologist, not a war college expert. Cut him some slack." Russell gave Dave a patronizing wink.

The chief of police sat up in his chair and leaned forward.

"What about an aerosol?"

"It's doubtful. But people have been known to catch rabies inhaling it in bat-infested caves," Dave said.

Soon the table became a free-for-all on the subject of how you could infect the population with rabies. Thirty or so possibilities were raised; Dave could shoot down some ideas, but for others it was less clear.

Paula raised her hand and stopped the discussion. She walked up to the Power Point presentation and pointed at the picture of Ben Curran. She faced the room.

"Look, we can theorize all we want on how they're going to do it, but I think the important thing is that we find Ben Curran. We find him. We stop what he's doing. It's as simple as that."

The men shifted in their chairs. Director Russell smiled and sat back down in his seat.

"You're right, Agent Mushari," Director Russell began. "Let's keep our eyes on the prize. Ben Curran is the key." Mr. Smith wiped some sweat from his brow and poured himself a glass of water.

"It's been done before." Mr. Smith brought the glass of water up to his eye to examine it. "It'll be done again."

The chief of police offered every resource available to them. In his mind, finding Ben Curran was the highest priority. He asked if they needed to involve the press in the manhunt. Mr. Smith looked over his glasses like the chief of police had just pantsed himself.

"Uh, no," Director Russell said diplomatically. "If they get wind that there's a terrorist operation that is so vague in its target, it could cause a national panic. So no leaks, ladies and gentlemen. It isn't going to help. Besides, if they know we're on to them it could speed up their plans." The chief of police cleared his throat.

"Of course. Now we'll start a canvassing operation borough by borough. We'll find out where this mutt is."

"Thank you, Chief. Every bit of help is appreciated. Let's get to it."

Dave stood up, stretched, and found himself facing Mr. Smith. Smith offered a limp, clammy handshake.

"So you're the new kid on the block," Mr. Smith said, containing a smile.

"I guess so."

"Look forward to working with you."

"Same here," Dave said warily.

"Rabies. This one's, well, a fresh take. And as you might suspect, I've heard them all."

Mr. Smith disappeared out the door. Paula walked up to Dave and nudged him. He looked around at her.

"You made a new friend," she said.

"Then why do I feel like I need to take a bath?"

Pearson strode up to them and looked between them.

"Why don't you follow me? I've got your temporary offices set up."

Pearson handed them their FBI passes, and Dave and Paula slung them around their necks.

They went down one floor and were shown offices with views of the New York skyline. The offices were sparsely furnished, but Dave and Paula couldn't help but feel important. Dave was happy to have an office above ground again. His descent from a corner office at the CDC to the basement had been harder on him than he wanted to admit. Just having a window again gave him hope. Maybe he'd turned a corner. Dave thought about what Paula had said about a man picking his destiny rather than the other way around. He wasn't sure she was right. He figured it was just luck that Dr. Root had given him the assignment. But luck had a habit of running out. When you live a life built on luck, crashing and burning was a natural by-product. At least that's what he had thought in his lowest moments. Maybe he was wrong. Maybe people go through dark periods that don't seem to end and then miraculously rise from the ashes.

Dave and Paula didn't spend much time in their new surroundings. They were dragged into meeting after meeting to brief department heads that ranged from the transit authority to the New York public school system. The only stumbling block was how the terrorists would implement their plan. Dave could only guess, and if he guessed wrong, he'd end up sending the whole law enforcement community on a wild goose chase. He had to be certain. He had to know. But how does a person get in the mind of a terrorist?

Dave's voice became hoarse, so he rested in the break room. He saw an agent with a stack of photos of Ben Curran. It was a combination of the mall photo and a pair of pictures from his life in Idaho.

A pair of NYPD cops followed the agent into the break room where the pair sealed the pictures inside a manila envelope and one of them tucked it under his arm.

"When are you starting the canvass?" the agent said.

"Few hours."

"Got a wire photo coming in from the ATF. I'll get that to you as soon as it comes in."

"Thanks."

Dave watched the cops head back out into the hallway and back to their precinct.

The agent headed out, leaving Dave alone in the break room. Out in the hall, people rushed back and forth. Dave knew it was all about the White Sleeper.

Paula passed the door, looked in, and walked over to Dave.

"You okay?" she asked.

"I hope they know what they're doing," he said.

"What do you mean?"

"It's just that this has become a committee operation. And committees can screw up worse than, well, two people."

"We couldn't exactly keep this to ourselves."

Dave laughed, and Paula put her hand on his shoulder. Dave felt calmed by her touch.

"We'll just have to keep doing what we've been doing, and we'll get them," she said.

Dave nodded, but his mind was still buzzing. How was Ben Curran going to do it? How had he figured out how to weaponize rabies? Dave knew in his heart of hearts that he was the one who had to figure it out. Paula was certainly capable, but he was the one who'd always been so good at finding things that were hiding in plain sight. He hoped that he could take that skill and apply it successfully here.

CHAPTER 26

Ben was informed that the package hadn't arrived yet. The Arabs were efficient in most cases. He couldn't let this fall apart. This was his destiny. The feds needed to know he wasn't some anonymous man whom they could toss aside as though he didn't exist.

The idea for his plan was, in truth, not his own. It was the subject of chapter eleven in the obscure spy novel he'd been reading. In some ways it had become Ben's bible. He had been in a used bookstore in Greenwich Village when a book fell off a shelf and landed at his feet. He picked it up, read the back cover, and was immediately intrigued. As time went on, he found the book helpful. Ben was positive that the book's appearance at his feet was part of a divine plan. It was God sending him a message to follow a journey, and the novel was his map.

Ben wandered through New York, waiting for the word that the package had arrived and he could pick it up. He had arranged a series of calls at various phone booths around the city. That was still the most secure way of conducting clandestine activities. Though the throwaway cell phones were hard to trace, phone booths were even harder for the NSA. You could use one and disappear into the city like a ghost.

Ben went to three appointed phone booths over three hours. He picked up a ringing phone on Fifty-second Street. Oren was on the other end.

"The package is caught in traffic."

"What?"

"There's a pileup on the expressway."

"There can't be any more delays. You can't afford more failures."

Oren was silent on the other end. He knew Ben was right. For all the bluster that Al Qaeda had levied on the Unites States, they hadn't had a successful strike within the United States since 9/11. When America was asleep, it was an easy target. Now, with the United States even half awake, striking it seemed insurmountable. That's why most of the successful operations were occurring out of the country.

"Call me at the next site," Oren said.

"Good-bye." Ben slammed the phone down. A slow, steady rain began to fall, and Ben cursed his lack of an umbrella. His next stop was five blocks uptown, and he'd get drenched. He was nursing a cold and decided he'd risk worsening it by sprinting in the downpour.

Ben arrived at the next phone early, so he stopped into a bodega to keep warm and shake out his wet clothes. He was looking at some magazines in a corner when he saw a pair of uniformed officers come into the shop.

The first cop was loud and moved up to the Chinese shopkeeper.

"Yo, Wang," he blurted out. "Got a guy we're looking for. You seen him?" The second cop showed him a picture. From where Ben stood he couldn't see the picture, but he had a bad feeling. His fear became so palpable he thought he might actually pass out. The Chinese shop owner looked over the first cop's shoulder and made Ben. He recognized him from the picture. Ben stood there frozen. All was lost. The Chinese shopkeeper would extend his long, bony finger and point to him, and he'd be arrested. Everything that Ben had dreamed of and planned for would go down the drain. He couldn't understand how the simple act of coming in out of the rain could decimate his plans.

What Ben didn't know was the shopkeeper had been shot twice in two robberies in the last four years. Neither of the shooters was ever captured, and the NYPD had been less than helpful. Ben was directly behind the cops; if he did point at him, there was likely to be gunplay. He looked at the cops innocently and said, "No, I never seen that guy. What he do?"

Ben sighed with relief. He quietly exited the bodega and crossed the street, dodging traffic and putting as much distance between himself and the street cops as he could.

As Ben headed to the next phone booth, he realized things were far worse than he thought. The feds were on an active hunt for him. He was certain it was Oren's fault. He had tried to kill an FBI agent and failed. Now the authorities had probably put some of the pieces together. But it wasn't too late. If he could get the package, he could still slip away.

The rain finally subsided. Ben reached the phone booth at his appointed time and picked up the ringing phone.

"It's arrived," Oren said confidently. "Where do you want to pick it up?"

"Home base."

"Okay."

"Is everybody there?"

"Yes."

"Good. This is an important day. We will need to celebrate."

"Of course. See you soon." And with that, the phone clicked dead. Ben ducked down into the subway and headed back toward his old apartment building.

Ben chose to avoid the elevator and took the steps up to his apartment building. No one used them, and he didn't want to be forced into an awkward conversation with a neighbor. He reached his floor and made sure there was no one in sight. He knocked on the Arabs' door. Khalid opened it and gave Ben a bear hug. Ben pushed him aside and closed the door. Oren stood beside a package that was sitting on a counter. It was a gray box sealed with white tape.

"Is that it?"

"Yes. Enough to kill upwards of a quarter of a million."

"Good work."

"Sorry about the delay."

"It doesn't matter now. We're ready. There any tea?"

"Certainly."

Ben went to a desk and slid the drawer open. He looked down into it and smiled.

Oren turned toward the teapot on the hot plate but never reached it. Ben had whipped out a silenced 9mm Glock. It was in the desk among a small stash of weapons. Ben put a bullet into the back of Oren's head. Assir looked up, but before he could react, Ben had put two bullets in his heart. When Khalid charged Ben, he emptied the remainder of the bullets into Khalid's body.

Ben grabbed Oren's legs, dragged his body into the bathroom, and deposited it in the tub. He did the same with Assir and Khalid. He stuffed them together in a pile. He washed the blood off his hands in the sink and sneezed. His saliva sprayed onto the mirror, and he cursed having to run through a rainstorm.

Ben closed the door and crossed to the package. He opened it with a knife and found it packed with vial after vial of the rabies virus. The box was heavier than it looked. He detached the silencer from his gun and tucked both into his jacket.

Ben quietly opened the door and heard someone coming down the hall toward the elevator. He waited until he was certain that they had boarded and then headed out into the hallway. Ben slipped down the stairs with ease. No one spotted him, and he was soon on the wet streets of the city, hailing a cab. He had considered going on the subway, but he worried the cops might be waiting for him there.

The cabs kept racing past him, filled with passengers. It was always harder to get one when it was raining. He opted to distance himself from his apartment building and briskly walked four city blocks uptown.

The street seemed less busy there.

A sense of freedom surged through Ben. He would no longer have to pretend that he respected the Arabs and had their hopes in his heart. Ben knew from the minute he sat down with Oren that he was going to kill him. He knew he was going to kill them all, but in Tunis's case, the FBI beat him to it. Ben felt that his father must be looking down on him and smiling. He was about to be more successful than his father, and Ben was certain that would have suited Harlan just fine; every father wants his son to be more successful than he.

When Ben was nearly picked up by the NYPD forty minutes earlier, he thought that his plans were over. But his escape had increased his belief that God was guiding him. God was on his side as he'd always been.

Ben hailed a cab two blocks down on the other side of the street. The cab swerved through traffic, cutting off a honking

FedEx truck. The wet streets softened the sounds of the tires as the taxi came to a screeching stop.

Ben hopped in the cab and closed the door, holding the sealed box tightly under his arm. The cabbie turned on his meter and didn't bother to look back at Ben.

"Where you headed?"

"Grand Central."

"There's an accident on the regular route. Gotta work around it. Might cost you an extra ten."

"I'm in no rush."

"I don't want you to think I'm cheating you or nothing."

"I trust you."

Ben leaned back, sitting sideways and taking up all the room. The cab driver punched the gas, zoomed off, and headed into thick traffic. Ben thought it amusing that the cabbie had no idea that he had a box that could kill as many people as a single modest-yield atomic bomb.

CHAPTER 27

Heidi Burns was, at first blush, the dream girl for most red-blooded males. She was blonde and five foot nine, with a healthy pair of surgically enhanced breasts. She had a perfect Nordic face with lips that seemed slightly plumped. She was also engaging and sexy. But the downside of Heidi was her temper. Her temper could bubble over in an instant. Growing up, she realized that when you're a ten, you should be treated better than less fortunate women. She met Khalid in a Middle Eastern restaurant where they struck up a conversation. Heidi had never dated a foreigner, but this handsome, olive-skinned Arab tempted her. Heidi decided to go for a one-night stand, but that stretched into a weekend date in her Upper West Side condo. Khalid was talented in the bedroom. Khalid also treated her well and lavished her with gifts. Heidi felt she had struck gold with Khalid and dared hope that it might become something permanent.

But it had been three days since she had heard from him. Her anger began to boil. Heidi would not and could not be ignored. She was now standing outside of Khalid's building with rage coursing through her body. She marched into the elevator and arrived on his floor. She stomped down the hall like a petulant child and began knocking on the door loudly.

"Khalid!" she screamed. "Khalid, you bastard, open the door!"

A woman peeked out of the apartment at the end of the hall. Heidi heard the door crack open.

"What the hell are you looking at? Close your damn door!"

The woman slammed the door shut. Heidi continued banging on the door with increasing ferocity.

"Open up! I said, open up!"

There was nothing but silence inside the apartment. Heidi rammed the door with her shoulder. She hit the door again and again.

"Open up, you bastard!"

Heidi put everything into it, and the door broke open. She marched into the apartment. A distinct and putrid odor hit her, but she didn't know what to make of it.

Heidi checked the window and looked out on the fire escape but then turned her attention to the bathroom. Heidi flung the door open and was instantly hit with the smell of rotting flesh. She saw the bloated heap of bodies and recognized Khalid's distorted body on top. Heidi stumbled backward, screaming. She slipped on the door frame to the bathroom and fell. She scrambled backward like a crab and looked out the broken front door to see a thick, young black man wearing hip hop gear who was carrying groceries. He stood in the hallway and looked in.

"I didn't do it," Heidi insisted. "I found them like that. Oh my God!"

The man put down his groceries and helped Heidi up. He was a paramedic and prided himself on his ability to handle difficult situations. He smelled the human decay and checked inside the bathroom; he jumped back as quickly as she had.

"Goddamn, what the hell happened in here?"

"I didn't do it."

He calmed her down and took her to his apartment across the hall. He called 911, and within fifteen minutes the place was crawling with cops.

The cops tried to question her, and it took a half an hour to assure her that they didn't think she was a suspect.

Officer McKenna, a dark-haired Irish American woman from Queens, questioned Heidi. She had a soothing demeanor that calmed the panicked Heidi.

"How long had you dated him?" McKenna asked gently.

"I dunno, four months."

"Did you meet any of his friends?"

"No, he didn't want me to."

"Why not?"

"I think he was embarrassed by his living circumstances," she said, drying her red eyes.

"So, he was poor?" McKenna queried.

"Oh no, he always had money. Lots of it. "

McKenna went into the hallway with her partner, Jake Ward, a jarhead who generally went along with whatever McKenna thought was prudent.

"Three dead Arabs in a bathtub and about twenty thousand in cash stuffed in a closet."

When McKenna had come across the cash, she knew something was up. She had been part of the recent canvass for Ben Curran, and they'd been advised at every roll call that there might be an Arab terrorist connection.

"I gotta go down to the car," she said.

She headed downstairs to her cruiser. When she reached the front door, she saw the press swarming outside. She wondered who told them about the murders.

McKenna was peppered with questions, but she avoided answering them. She opened the trunk and took out the metal clipboard she used for writing up reports. She had left it there the evening before and had forgotten to retrieve it.

McKenna made her way through the throngs of neighbors and press and headed back upstairs in a sprint. She arrived back on the floor, almost knocking over the coroner.

"Hey, watch where you're going."

"Yeah, yeah, yeah, sorry."

She looked for her partner, who was giving an update into the hand mic clipped to his shoulder.

"Where's the super?" McKenna asked.

Her partner pointed to the manager. McKenna approached him.

"I'm Officer McKenna. Can I ask you a few questions?"

"Yeah, yeah. What?"

McKenna had a rubber band around her metal clipboard, and she yanked it off without looking. She reached in and pulled out a picture of Ben Curran and handed it to him.

"Have you ever seen this man?"

"He's my renter down the hall. Used to see him hanging with the dead Arabs sometimes," the manager said indifferently.

"Could I see his room?"

The manager grumbled and pulled out his keys. McKenna entered the apartment and found it stripped of everything but the furniture. It reeked of bleach, and McKenna assumed Curran had scrubbed the place down before he left.

"You seen enough? " the manager said. McKenna nodded and stepped back out into the hallway.

McKenna took out her cell phone and nervously dialed a number. When the hunt for Ben Curran started, every officer had been issued a direct number to the chief. If they came across what he termed "a hot connection to the case," they were to call him directly.

The phone rang three times, and the chief answered.

"Yes."

"Officer McKenna, sir. Seventh precinct. Uh, well, I got three dead Arabs and twenty thousand in cash in this Lower East Side apartment. The apartment manager confirmed Ben Curran was their neighbor and knew them."

"He ID'd him?"

"Yes sir."

"You get in Curran's room?"

"Yes sir. No sign of him. Doubt if we'll even find a fingerprint."

"You think he killed his cell partners?"

McKenna hadn't known this involved a terror cell until the chief misspoke, and she just played along as though she were in the loop.

"I think that's a solid conclusion, sir."

"McKenna, I'm coming right down."

The chief made it across town in forty-five minutes and was escorted into the bathroom by McKenna. The chief had seen more than his share of bodies and acted unaffected by the potent stench.

He recognized Oren's face. The chief had recently been privy to a gallery of photos of terrorist suspects that they'd been trying to track down. Oren was one of them.

"Good work, McKenna."

The chief was on the phone to Director Russell in an instant. Russell picked up his cell and was at first annoyed by the intrusion, but that swiftly changed as the chief spoke.

"Director Russell. I think we've got a lead on this thing. One of my officers pulled it together."

"What kind of lead?" Director Russell said, not believing that the NYPD could turn anything up before the FBI could.

"We found Curran's apartment and the sleeper cell."

"How can you be sure?"

"The super ID'd him, and we have three dead Arabs—foreign nationals in the apartment next to him," the chief said.

"Did the press get wind?"

"Yeah, multiple homicides have that tendency. But they don't know about Curran."

Director Russell didn't like the chief's tone, but he needed him on his side.

"Well, good work, chief."

The chief hung up and smiled confidently. He looked at McKenna and gently punched her in the arm.

"You made my day, McKenna. Love to show up the FBI."

CHAPTER 28

Dave and Paula stood in Ben's apartment. There were no clues. Ben wasn't a fool. In fact, when she checked his high school files, she found he was straight-A student. He had even been offered a place in a gifted program, but he'd declined.

"So this guy's got something going on upstairs?"

"Beyond his twisted mania, he's out-of-the-park brilliant. He's clearly a manipulator. Guy suckered a whole terror cell into working for him."

"So he's going to be unconventional in how he does this?" Dave said.

"Yeah, your boss is convinced he's going to use an aerosol. Get planes and spray rabies all over the city."

"You don't buy it?"

"No. He's not a fool. He scrubbed the place down. I bet he's not even in the city. He must know we're hunting for him."

Director Russell, flanked by his underlings, breezed into the room. He moved up to Paula, who gave him an update.

"Any idea how long he's been gone?"

"The morbidity indicates they died three days ago, so he could have made some serious tracks," Dave said.

Director Russell said nothing more and wandered into the hallway.

CHAPTER 29

Mrs. Kellogg's eyes had been open for at least an hour. She had been asleep for days while recovering from the plague. She realized that she was alive, and prayed that her husband and children were too. She looked up to see Dr. Dunn.

Outside the sealed room, he put on a surgical mask, came in, and approached Mrs. Kellogg's bed.

"You're awake."

Mrs. Kellogg looked at him hopefully and managed to ask, "What about my kids?"

"They're asleep but recovering nicely."

Her throat was dry, so she took a sip of water from a cup that rested on the side table. She swallowed slowly then asked, "And my husband?"

"He's weak but okay. It's been slower for him."

"What happened to us?"

Dr. Dunn sighed heavily and stepped closer to her.

"You all had a very close call. I'm afraid you contracted the bubonic plague."

"What?'

"It's also known as the black death."

"How did we get bubonic plague?"

"Well, it's not clear. It has something to do with your trip to New York."

"I got it in New York?"

"Yes, but we're not sure how. The CDC found some traces in the mall."

"Oh my God!"

"Do you have any idea how you could have contracted it from the mall?"

"No, of course not. How in the world do you get a disease in a mall?"

"I know. Everyone's stumped."

"You do everything right in your life, and this happens. We go to church, take care of ourselves. I mean, we even got flu shots in New York for the whole family."

"Excuse me?"

"We got flu shots."

"Why'd you do it on the trip?"

"Well, when we told the young man that we were from Arkansas, he pointed out we could get the flu from the recirculated air on the plane back."

"What young man?"

"The one giving the free flu shots in the mall."

Dr. Dunn blinked a moment.

"You got free flu shots?"

"Yes, is there something wrong, Doctor?

"The Munsens and the Henrys, too?"

"Yes. Better safe than sorry. That's what I always say."

Mrs. Kellogg watched Dr. Dunn rush out of the sealed room. She could see him pick up a phone and dial.

PART THREE

DARK TRUTH

CHAPTER 30

Dave was sitting in Director Russell's office. Russell and Pearson were going over some information as Dave tried to desperately figure out how the pieces were fitting together. He sat on the couch as Paula entered, excited.

"We got IDs on two of the guys."

She pulled out two pictures, one of Khalid and the other of Assir.

"Assir's been on the watch list. No idea how the guy got in the country."

Paula spoke, but Dave wasn't listening. The Arabs were dead, and he felt it wouldn't lead back to Ben. He was too careful, too smart. His own personal doubts rose within him. Then his cell phone rang.

"Dr. Richards."

It was the familiar voice of Dr. Dunn.

"Dr. Dunn. How are the patients?"

"Well, that's why I'm calling. Mrs. Kellogg woke up. She told me something that might be important."

"What's that?"

"Did you know about the free flu shots?"

"What free flu shots?"

"The ones they had in the mall in New York."

Paula, Russell, and Pearson looked at Dave and realized something serious was going on.

"Say that again?" Dave said.

"The three families. They all had flu shots in the mall. Some young man administered them."

"Sonofabitch. Thank you, Dr. Dunn. I'll be in touch."

Dave hung up and shook his head. Russell rose and looked at Dave for the update. Dave stood.

"What was that all about, Dr. Richards?"

"Ben Curran gave the test subjects free flu shots in the mall. That's what was going on in the waiting area. I bet if you showed Mrs. Kellogg the picture of Curran you'd have an ID."

"Pearson, get on that." Pearson ran out of the room.

"What does this mean, Doctor?"

"I never bought the aerosol idea. But like you said, I'm not from a war college. I just couldn't figure out how they got sick and how he was going to take the plan into action."

"Flu shots," Paula said, getting it.

"It's diabolical. You lace a flu shot with rabies, and it's in your system without you knowing it. Two weeks go by, and by the time you realize something's wrong, it's too late."

"Christ," Russell said.

"You were right, Paula. This guy is smart," Dave said.

"He's going to poison the flu-dose supply?"

"It's flu season. You realize how many doses are being given out across the country just today?"

"Doctor, I can't go out and tell the world that the flu shot supply has been exposed to rabies. It would start a national panic!"

"I know! And he knows. We gotta figure out how he's going to do it. Or maybe he's done it already."

"He goes to a doctor's office. Infects it there?" Russell said.

"Too small," Paula said. "This guy wants to do something spectacular. He feels the federal government wronged him, and he wants payback."

"She's right. The planning is too detailed and too extensive to be that simple. It's big. I mean, he went as far as to kill his partners to protect his plan."

"Maybe he didn't like that they tried to kill us. Trying to kill a federal agent brought a lot more heat down on them. "

"Yeah, that probably didn't go over well. No doubt he saw it as sloppy. But it's more than that. Paula's right. He's figured out some exotic attack."

Dave got up from the couch, headed to Russell's seat, and urged him out of it.

"Could you move, sir?"

Russell got up. Dave sat down, turned on Russell's computer, and got on the Internet. He typed furiously, and a screen popped up.

"What are you doing?" Russell asked.

"Remember the flu-dose shortage a few years back?"

"Yeah."

"There was one manufacturer, and it was somewhere in England."

Dave googled some articles and found the name of the company. Dave looked satisfied and sat back in Russell's chair, looking at Paula and Russell.

"Titan Technologies. That's got to be it. If he could get to the source of where the flu doses are made, he could kill hundreds of thousands. Possibly millions."

"And we can't tell them to stop shipping because it would cause a whole other set of deaths during flu season."

"For him it's a win-win. We have to catch him. He could already be in England."

"Can't be. He's on all the watch lists at the airports," Paula said.

"You're underestimating him," Dave answered back. Paula looked slightly hurt. "I'm sorry. That's true he is on the watch lists. But look at what this guy has done."

"He could have gotten around the lists. He could have hired a plane for all we know," Russell said while looking out his window. Paula walked up to the director.

"I trust Dr. Richard's instincts, sir."

"We better get ourselves to London," Russell said, looking back at both of them.

"Agent Mushari, gather the agents on the case," Russell ordered.

"And Paula."

"Yes sir."

"Tell my assistant to get Channing Zumwalt on the phone."

Dave looked at his cell phone and dialed Dr. Root's phone number. It rang, and then his voice mail picked up. Dave was about to speak when Russell asked him a question. Dave hung up.

"How is a flu vaccine made?"

Dave went into an involved discussion of the process, and by the time he was finished, Channing Zumwalt was waiting to be briefed via speakerphone. In all the excitement, Dave forgot the initial call to Dr. Root.

CHAPTER 31

The Omni International Hotel in Atlanta wasn't the finest hotel in the city, but it was comfortable. The rooms were well appointed, and the service was exemplary. The restaurant on the ground level was called Fiore's and had attained one Michelin star. It was Dr. Evan Lussier's favorite restaurant, and he decided to celebrate some good news by taking his assistant Maureen to lunch. The good news was that his raise had been approved by Washington. Lussier and Maureen had been having an affair for the last seven months, so lunch would be followed by a trip to a secluded suite in the north tower of the hotel.

Maureen was short, exotic-looking, and everything Lussier's wife wasn't. Maureen understood all Lussier's quirks and never scolded him. She was sexy, but not to the point that other women were jealous of her.

He felt that Maureen was what a wife should be: elegant and poised in public and wild in the bedroom. He hadn't been very happy with his wife Freda. Freda had many interests, and Lussier wasn't one of them. His wife's indifference had gnawed at him until he hired Maureen. From the first there was an obvious kinetic energy between them that finally exploded during a bioterrorism conference at the Hay-Adams Hotel in DC.

That first time, Lussier and Maureen made love in a room that was a short walk from the White House. He had never cheated on his wife before, but he didn't have any regrets. He felt a man in his position deserved a mistress. When his contemporaries had bragged about the women they had stashed around the country, Lussier had been jealous. All he had was Freda, and she wasn't interested in him. In some ways Lussier didn't mind. She had taken to the fried Southern diet and had let herself go. He had been resigned to his mediocre personal life until he met Maureen. Now he had the career he wanted, the upscale life, and the woman on the side. Lussier bragged to his friends that his life was perfect.

Lussier examined Maureen's alabaster body as she slept. He felt like a conquering gladiator as he stood over her. Her eyes opened, and she smiled.

"That was nice," Maureen said, rolling over on her stomach.

"A personal best," Lussier said, laughing.

"We going on any trips soon? I'd sure like to get out of town."

"Nothing on the horizon."

Maureen smiled briefly and began to put her clothes back on. She went into the bathroom and fixed her hair and makeup. She made sure that there were no signs of the affair. She would regularly check his clothes for lipstick and hair and even had him bring a spare shirt to the office in case there was a mistake. That created a strong trust with Lussier. Lussier liked that she wasn't angling to become the next Mrs. Lussier. She was angling to be the other woman for the duration. This was a perfect situation for him. As far as he was concerned, life couldn't possibly get any better.

"Evan."

"Yeah, dear," Lussier said while putting on a sock.

"That guy from the NSA called. Did you call him back?"

"NSA? Why do they want to talk to me?"

"Don't know, honey."

"Who was it?"

Maureen appeared out of the bathroom looking impeccable. Her every move made Lussier salivate. She pulled out her Blackberry and checked the messages.

"Zumwalt."

"Channing Zumwalt?"

"Christ, Maureen, that's not NSA; that's the national security advisor. Works right beside the president."

Maureen just batted her eyelashes and shifted her elegant frame. She knew there'd be no retribution for her mistake. She wetted her lips and sat next to him on the bed.

"I'm sorry."

"It's all right. But I'd better give him a call." Lussier dressed, picked up his cell phone, and dialed Zumwalt's office. He waited as a series of assistants kept telling him to stand by. He was told that Zumwalt was on Air Force One flying over Montana. Then after a few moments, Zumwalt was on the phone.

"Evan."

"Channing, how are you?"

"Not bad. Had a nice talk with one of your boys."

"One of my boys?"

"Dr. Dave Richards."

Lussier went silent. He could only imagine that Dr. Richards had a relapse and had told off the national security advisor in a drunken tirade. Lussier fought off a panic attack and took a deep breath. He wasn't sure what to say. He couldn't imagine how Dr. Richards could have come in contact with someone so high up. He slightly stuttered as he spoke.

"Dr. Dave Richards?"

"Yes. He briefed me on the White Sleeper business."

Lussier couldn't even begin to imagine what a white sleeper was. He wondered if he had missed a memo.

"How are things proceeding?" He didn't want to let on that he was completely out of the loop. He knew Dave had gone to Arkansas and then later New York, but that was the extent of it. His final instructions to Dr. Root had been to cut Dr. Richards loose. He never followed up. He assumed that Dr. Richards had gone back to his hideout for the remainder of his tenure. But obviously, he hadn't.

"Well, they connected the terror cell with Ben Curran, and we've been trying to figure out how they are going to distribute." Lussier wanted to ask, "Distribute what?" but deliberately decided not to ask. Again, he knew nothing of what was going on and wished he were in his office where he could order subordinates to bring him up to speed. Instead, he was half naked in a suite at the Omni International Hotel.

"Richards seems to think England is the action point. I think they're leaving tonight."

"That would seem prudent."

"We have our CIA station chief working with MI6 in London to see what they can nail down before they arrive."

"This, of course, is consuming a lot of my time and I need to get back to it," Lussier said.

"Oh, of course. If you need any help from the executive branch don't hesitate to call."

Zumwalt hung up, and Lussier dialed Dr. Root. He was in such a fury it made even Maureen nervous. Lussier turned crimson, and Maureen placed a hand on his shoulder to calm him. Lussier wriggled away. Dr. Root picked up the phone.

"Root here."

"Dr. Root, what the hell is going on with Richards?"

"What do you mean?"

"The guy's been briefing Channing Zumwalt, and I don't know a damn thing about it. What the hell are you guys doing?"

"I haven't talked to Dr. Richards in days. Where'd you hear this from?"

"Channing Zumwalt. They're working on something called 'the White Sleeper.' What the hell is the White Sleeper? I felt like a goddamn ass talking to the national security advisor about something I didn't know anything about. What if the president had goddamn called me? I would have been sitting here like a buffoon. Did you know about this?"

"I'm just as in the dark as you are."

"This is bullshit, Root! Bullshit!"

"Look, let me get in contact with Dr. Richards."

"No, no, don't say a word to him. You understand?"

"Yes sir. But sir."

"What?"

"Dr. Richards may be in the middle of something substantial. Don't you think that letting him go now might be...unwise."

"I'll tell you what's unwise. Dr. Richards is running an operation and keeping me out of the loop. He's trying to get back at me, and no one does that!"

Dr. Lussier hung up and turned to Maureen.

"You gotta get me on the next flight to New York." Maureen helped him on with his coat and told him to head to the airport. She'd have everything arranged by the time he got there.

Dr. Lussier was rattled to the core as he pulled himself together and jogged out of the room in his signature loping gait. He came up to the elevator and pounded the button. When he got on, he punched the lobby button so hard the tiny light inside it broke. He mumbled to himself. A man got on the elevator but stood as far away from Lussier as possible, as if Lussier were deranged.

Dr. Richards had encroached on Lussier's world. Politics. Lussier feared that Dave was destroying his reputation behind his back. Lussier had never suspected that Dr. Richards, that lush, was a threat.

Lussier launched himself out of the elevator and shoved a room-service waiter out of his way. He cut in line to get his car from the valet and was soon speeding to the airport. He cursed himself for not gassing up his car. The needle was teetering on empty, but Lussier managed to get to the appropriate terminal and found, as Maureen had promised, that all the arrangements had been taken care of. Maureen was invaluable to Lussier in many ways, not just as a lover. She was efficient and made him look more professional. He didn't know all the particulars of what was going on, but he knew he'd need her with him.

"Follow me up there tomorrow."

"Anything you say, boss."

"Thanks, Maureen."

Lussier closed his cell phone and sensed that he was developing feelings for Maureen. He really did care about her, but he couldn't let her know that. He had his life in order, and falling in love with Maureen would mean total chaos.

Dr. Evan Lussier boarded the American Airlines flight for JFK and took a random seat. He didn't much care for coach, but this was an emergency and he was sure that Maureen had wisely picked the first flight to New York.

As he settled into his seat, he realized he hadn't even told his wife he was headed out of town. He'd call when he got into the city. As the plane lifted skyward, he thought she probably wouldn't notice that he was gone. Maybe he should test his theory and not call.

Now he needed to find out what was going on without anyone discovering he'd been in the dark. Lussier placed a call with the phone slotted right in front of him at his seat. He reached his friend right away, and by the time the conversation was over, Lussier had elicited not only information about the White Sleeper, but a promise to keep the call a secret.

CHAPTER 32

Dave grabbed his files and stuffed them into his briefcase. It was mostly filled with random reports sent to him by the various agencies that littered the government landscape. Everyone wanted to be ready to share in his success. Dave tried to keep abreast of it all. Now that his opinion was valuable, he wanted to make sure he knew what he was talking about.

Paula rapped on the outer edge of his open door.

"You ready?"

"Yeah, I guess so. When are we leaving?"

"In a couple of hours. They had to switch jets."

"What about my passport? It's at home."

"Dave, we won't be going through customs."

Dave's face turned red. He wasn't used to this cloak-and-dagger side of government. He had been briefed that MI6 was working with them, and in that world passports didn't exist.

"So we won't officially be in the UK?"

"Not really."

"You think I'm right? I mean you think this is how Curran is going to do it?"

"It makes sense. Security is nonexistent in these places."

Dave sat back and stared out over the brilliant night lights of New York. He'd finally gotten a good night's sleep, but he was still tired. He'd been assaulted with information for days. He figured that he'd catch some sleep on the plane, until an assistant slid a piece of paper into his inbox. It detailed the topics to be discussed on the flight to the Royal Air Force base just outside Iver Heath, Buckinghamshire.

Paula sat on the hard couch and looked at him.

"What?" Dave asked.

"You never talk about your wife."

"Huh?"

"I mean, I see the ring on your finger."

Dave twisted the gold band, looked down at it, and then looked up self-consciously.

"Divorced?" she said quietly.

"Separated."

"But you didn't want to."

"No. It was my fault."

"So it's over."

Dave looked at his ring mournfully.

"I guess so."

Paula slipped out of the room and made her way down the hallway. Dave was gazing out over the skyline when he heard a voice behind him.

"Dr. Richards."

Dave slowly turned and saw the gawky figure of Dr. Evan Lussier loping into his office. Dave was speechless at the sight of Lussier. He couldn't believe he was in New York. He felt a simmering rage toward Lussier for firing him but decided to cap it.

"Dr. Lussier."

"Well, you've been busy."

"Just taking care of loose ends."

"Loose ends? You call this a loose end?"

"I suppose it depends on how you look at it."

"I'm the director of counterterrorism, and you kept me in the dark."

"You fired me."

Dr. Lussier's face became flushed, and he closed the door behind him.

"You're just trying to show me up. You're just trying to get back at me. You think if you make me look incompetent you'll get your job back?"

"You don't need my help to look incompetent."

Dave wished he hadn't said that. It was sure to come back and bite him in the ass. He considered Lussier to be nothing but a political hack. Dave knew his boss was trained as a surgeon, but Lussier's professors at Ohio State had advised him against practicing. He wasn't good enough to be cutting open human beings. He had the ego and the temper of a surgeon but not the skill. Lussier resorted to using his medical degree to rise in the ranks of civil service, something to which he was well suited.

Dr. Lussier leaned into him. Dave could see Lussier's veins actually throbbing in his forehead.

"You aren't going to England on that flight."

"What are you talking about?"

"I'm head of CDC counterterrorism, and you're on your way out. I'll take your place in England."

"You don't know anything about this! This is a critical situation. This isn't about office politics! It's bigger than your ego. This is about saving lives, maybe hundreds of thousands."

"And I'm taking the credit," Lussier said plainly. "I've already spoken to Director Russell and made your apologies. Now I need all your files so I can get up to speed."

"You think you can get a PhD in toxicology in the next two hours?"

Lussier took the file from Dave's hands, opened the door, and marched across the floor.

Dave sighed. He'd nearly pulled it off, and now Lussier was going to run with the ball and quite possibly screw it up. And if he did, he'd certainly figure out how to blame it on Dave.

The flight for the United Kingdom took off without Dr. David Richards on board. The idea of hanging out in his FBI office seemed counterproductive. His mission was, for all intents and purposes, over. Lussier had shoved him aside. Dave had enjoyed feeling like the wonder boy again. He enjoyed everyone looking to him for the answers, and he wasn't ready to return to obscurity. Dave felt it was just a cosmic tease. He was a soon-to-be ex-employee of the CDC after running point on the most important case since the anthrax attacks in 2001. In his heart he knew he'd be replaced sooner or later. But what really concerned him was that Lussier didn't send Dr. Root. Root was top in his field, and Lussier was merely a civil servant with a medical degree.

He went back to his hotel room and ordered room service. He thought of his Israeli roommate at Dartmouth and ordered two desserts.

The door started to open, and he assumed it was turndown service. But it was Paula. She looked uncharacteristically fragile.

"They felt my services weren't needed," Paula said, standing in the doorway. Paula walked over to Dave.

"Lussier?"

"Doesn't make sense. Lussier has no sway with Russell. Russell thinks Lussier is an obsequious sycophant," Paula said as she came into the room.

"Then why'd they take you off the case?'

"Why do you think? Look at me. They think I'm part of the problem. Not the solution. I'm an Arab," Paula said, sitting down next to him. She stifled a sob. Paula tamped it down so quickly Dave barely noticed.

"Come on. They wouldn't do that to you now. They've got to think you're invaluable."

"What else could it be? Pearson tells me I'm not needed at the airport. I'm standing there with my bags."

"If anything it's because you got lumped in with me. Sorry."

"Dave, I'll never be sorry that we met." She gave him a hug, and Dave held her tightly. She looked up at him, and he looked down at her. There was pain in her eyes. It seemed like an eternity, but finally he kissed her. Paula pulled back and instinctively looked at Dave's ring finger and saw the ring was missing. Paula looked back at him, and she kissed him back, shoving him gently back on the bed. Paula opened his shirt and kissed his chest.

Dave hadn't been with a woman in over a year, and he'd forgotten how good it felt. Dave noticed as he gripped her how firm her body was. He rolled on top of her, kissing her gently and opening her shirt. Paula gripped his broad shoulders. Paula unzipped his pants and slipped off his underwear. Paula undressed and got under the covers, and Dave followed eagerly. They made love for an hour until they collapsed in exhaustion.

They lay in silence for a few minutes. Paula looked over at him. Dave felt his despair waning. He couldn't take his eyes off Paula. He may have lost his career, but maybe he had gained something more.

"I wanted to do that for a long time," Paula confessed.

"Why didn't you?"

"Wedding ring. Not the home-wrecking type."

"That home was wrecked long ago," Dave said.

"Well, if you ask me," Paula said, tucking her body in closely to his, "she blew it."

"You didn't know me before."

"Sometimes you gotta wait for wine to reach its proper age." Paula smiled.

"Oh, I'm aged perfectly now?"

She kissed him and said, "Absolutely."

The phone rang, and Dave picked it up. The voice was vaguely familiar on the other end. It was Mr. Smith, the unofficial official.

"Dr. Richards."

"Mr. Smith."

Paula sat up in bed. She moved closer to Dave and tried to hear the conversation on the other end.

"Could you and Agent Mushari join me in the Blue Room?" Smith asked.

Paula looked at Dave, anxious to know what was going on. Dave remembered the Blue Room was the bar on the mezzanine level. He'd seen it listed but obviously chose not to spend any time there.

The phone clicked dead.

The Blue Room was bathed in blue luminescent light that gave the patrons an eerie look. A lone bartender was working, but the watering hole seemed otherwise empty. Dave wondered if it had been cleared out on purpose. Paula looked around; maybe the call had been a prank. But then the bald-headed Smith peeked around a secluded booth.

"Dr. Richards, Agent Mushari. Please join me."

And with that, he disappeared behind the high-backed booth. Dave and Paula shared a wary look and hesitantly walked toward Mr. Smith.

"Do I look like I just had sex?" Paula asked.

"Absolutely." Dave smiled. He smoothed her hair with his palm.

When they sat down, Dave noted that three club sodas were already at the table, with swizzle sticks all pointed in the same direction. Mr. Smith forced a smile and said, "In honor of your sobriety and your religion, Miss Mushari." Mr. Smith raised his glass to them.

"Very thoughtful," Dave said.

"I have my moments." Smith began his ritualistic wiping of his hands with his handkerchief. Paula watched warily. Smith looked up, catching Paula's gaze.

"It's an affliction," Smith said.

"Hyperhidrosis," Dave said. Smith cocked his head and finished wiping his hands for the time being.

"Well, you know about a little bit more than just toxicology, don't you, Dr. Richards?"

"A little," Dave said stifling a smile.

"I have what the civilians call sweaty palms," Smith said, directed toward Paula who was looking at him blankly.

"There's a surgical cure for that," Dave said in a professional tone. Smith leaned forward, grabbed his club soda, and took a small sip.

"Yes, read about it. But in my world I'm not trusting of anyone wanting to put a needle in me. I'm sure you understand my, well, reservations."

Paula was growing impatient and was certain that he hadn't appeared to ask medical advice about an obscure malady. She pushed her drink to the side.

"What's this about, Mr. Smith?" Paula asked.

"I hope you didn't feel singled out, Agent Mushari. I mean, being pulled off the flight this evening."

Mr. Smith smiled, and Paula tried to restrain herself.

"You had me pulled from the flight? Why?"

Dave put his hand on her, calming her down. Paula looked at him and sat back, trying to restrain herself.

"Why'd you do it, Smith?" Dave said.

"I needed the core team here."

"You did?"

"We believe you are right about how he's going to weaponize rabies. But we don't think he's in the United Kingdom.

"Then where is he?" Paula said. Mr. Smith took out his iPhone and looked up some information. He placed the phone down in front of them. Dave and Paula squeezed in together and looked at a report on Ben Curran. Dave quickly skimmed it; the subject was about something called FacIdent.

"What's FacIdent?" Dave asked.

"Facial recognition identification. It is an amazing tool in the war on terror. People in my world rely heavily on it. Now, we installed a search command for Mr. Curran's likeness around the time he left Idaho. We shouldn't have done that because, well, we legally can't be involved with domestic issues."

"Why would you have been interested in Ben Curran before he became the White Sleeper?" Paula inquired.

"Oh, it might be about mathematical probabilities," Smith said coyly. "When someone like Ben Curran appears on the scene, there is an increased possibility of an Oklahoma-type incident."

"But that's domestic," Dave reminded.

"Yes, the CIA is being very naughty getting its nose into places it shouldn't be. But if the CIA were effective in stopping a fellow like Ben, there might be more tolerance toward our involvement in…domestic affairs."

"Okay, great. You want to legally be involved in domestic spying," Paula started. "What's this FacIdent got to do with any of this?"

"Well, these FacIdents are positioned in many places. They are in places that, well, no one knows about. I couldn't give you any more details than that."

"Many places?" Paula asked.

"Many. Yes. But shhhh." He held his long, bony finger up to his lips and then chortled, obviously amused with himself.

"Don't try to find them. We've concealed them well."

"We don't want to find your secret eyes. We just want to know why you are trusting us," Dave said.

"Because you and Miss Mushari need a win. And if you reveal what I'm telling to you, your bosses will just take the credit and that will be that. And to be truthful, and I rarely am, you two have a higher likelihood of succeeding. The mathematical likelihood of Director Russell getting Ben Curran is quite low."

Dave had no doubt that Smith had actual calculations of success and failure probabilities. Dave had a mathematician friend from MIT who was working on probability programs for the feds. Maybe he'd designed the computer to do these calculations.

"Look, this isn't about getting credit. It isn't even about saving my job anymore," Dave said.

Smith looked at him with a broad grin and sat back in his seat. He looked at him with amazement.

"Dr. Richards, are you actually one of those people who puts the common good ahead of his self-interest?"

"Don't look so surprised. I'm sure there are more than you might think."

Dave looked embarrassed that he had made himself sound like a boy scout. But he didn't know any other way to respond.

Smith looked at Paula, who had been hanging on Dave's every word.

"And Agent Mushari, I take it you are cut from the same cloth."

"Yeah. Smith, there are a lotta lives on the line here. If we end up working in a Seven Eleven after this it doesn't matter to me."

"Well, I am sorry I put your motivations into such a cynical context," Smith said.

Smith took back his iPhone, slid his finger over the surface, and continued.

"The FacIdent system is in every airport, and we didn't get any hits on Ben Curran. Ergo, Mr. Curran is not in the United Kingdom plotting against us. He's here. Somewhere."

Paula leaned in closer, pushing her club soda aside. "Where is he?" Smith ran his finger up and down his iPhone, trying to find the screen he was searching for. He stopped and looked up at them.

"The last hit was picked up as Curran headed to Grand Central Station. Unfortunately, that's where the trail ends." Smith showed them video of Ben walking through Grand Central. Dave watched intently. He couldn't help but feel that Ben Curran didn't look like a diabolical domestic terrorist. Ben looked like the good-natured kid who bagged your groceries at the market and offered to help you take them out to your car.

Paula wasn't nearly as reflective and looked at Smith coolly.

"Why have you been sitting on this for four days?"

"FacIdent is in its nascent form. The sifting process is slow, and the data only came in this morning," Smith informed them. "You need to find him before the dolts come back from England. It's safe to assume that this is all on you two now. You've done an exemplary job so far. So keep up the good work. Of course I was never here, and you've never heard of FacIdent."

"Because the CIA would never spy on Americans," Paula said.

"Yes, that sort of business stopped in the seventies."

"Sounds like you're the one who needs the win," Dave said.

Smith looked at him coolly and wiped his hands. Dave waited for a response and never got one. Dave realized he had reached into a territory that was sensitive. Dave cleared his throat and decided not to press him further.

Dave looked around the room and saw that the Blue Room was still absent any other customers. He leaned in and said quietly, "You're leaving this completely in our hands. The whole thing?"

"You realize what you're doing?"

Smith finished his club soda and wiped his hands. He looked at his fingers and looked back at Dave.

"I have always had a very good eye for talent, Dr. Richards. You'll do just fine."

Mr. Smith rose and, without saying good-bye, left the Blue Room. Smith never said good-bye. It was his way. He would dispense his information and then disappear. That's how it had been all of his professional life. There was much to do being an unofficial official and the White Sleeper crisis was only one of the many things he had to tend to.

Paula looked at Dave, who was staring straight ahead.

"Can we, I mean, are we allowed to stay on this without our bosses knowing?"

"We can't afford not to. Besides, I don't have a boss anymore."

"Yeah, but I do."

"Well, then I guess we better not let it blow up in our faces."

"And if it does, do you think Smith's going to be there to pull our fannies out of the fire?"

"I think Smith and I had a connection. We're simpatico," Dave joked and drank his club soda.

"I'm not laughing, Dr. Richards. We've been dropped from the case, and Darth Vader is telling us to get back on it. Forgive me if I'm a little skeptical."

A few minutes after Smith left, people began filtering into the bar as though they'd been given the all-clear signal. Within several minutes there wasn't a seat to be had.

CHAPTER 33

Paula and Dave walked back to their room. Paula looked at Dave and started to say something but then got quiet. Dave instantly noticed. Paula had a look of stifled revulsion that made Dave self-conscious.

"What?"

"Nothing."

"What?"

"Uh, you've, well, become pitted. You need a bath." Dave smelled himself and realized he was reeking.

"Oh, sorry."

"Don't be. I'm kind of responsible. Gave you a workout."

Paula gave him a quick kiss.

Dave didn't want to admit their lovemaking hadn't been his source of perspiration. The truth was that their little meeting with Mr. Smith scared the hell out of him. Dave was usually talented at concealing fear, but his sweat and apocrine glands didn't always cooperate. The Mr. Smiths of the world were not the kind of people with whom you wanted to be involved. Dave feared that it wouldn't be the last time he met up with this black-bag operative. He didn't mind being recognized for his skills in the medical community, but being recognized in the CIA community made him feel uncomfortable. This was a world of double crosses and triple crosses. It was a world where everyone was expendable.

Dave excused himself and took an extended shower that went on a shade too long. He heard Paula knocking on the bathroom door telling him to hurry up. He threw on some black jeans and a black pullover sweater. It was the only things he had that were clean.

Dave came out of the bathroom and Paula looked him up and down, impressed.

"You look good."

He picked up the phone and asked the front desk to call for a taxi. Dave and Paula headed down to the lobby where a yellow cab was waiting. Dave tipped the doorman, and they got in.

"So where to?" asked the cabbie.

Dave looked at Paula.

"Grand Central?" Dave asked. Paula nodded, and the cab driver turned out into the light traffic.

Grand Central was the only lead they had. The trail had gone cold since Ben had disappeared into the mammoth train station. Paula had suggested they go there. They'd had luck before when they had followed the trail of the Arkansas church group and connected Ben Curran to the crimes. Paula hoped that approach would bring them the luck they desperately needed.

The cab pulled up in front of Grand Central. They stepped out and were hit by a cold gust that cut through them, reminding them that winter was just around the corner.

It was about ten in the evening, and Dave pulled his jacket tightly around him and looked at Paula.

"Smells like snow."

"What does that mean?"

"You never noticed that? Before it snows there's a certain smell."

"No, never noticed that." Paula set out ahead of him, and Dave paid the cabbie and moved to catch up to her.

They entered the giant expanse that was Grand Central. There were only a few trains leaving at this late hour, so there was a paucity of travelers. Dave noticed there was a distinct echo when they talked, so they moved behind the ticketing area where it seemed devoid of people.

Paula turned and faced Dave, confident no one could hear them.

"Okay, so he was here three days ago," she said.

"And he went somewhere. But where?"

"Check the video?"

"Yeah, let's start there."

They made their way up to the security office, and Paula showed her FBI credentials. To their surprise, they were met with some resistance from an officious security manager who wanted a court order before he would show them anything. He was an expert on corporate policy at the firm that handled security at Grand Central.

"Can you get your boss on the phone?"

"He'd have the same answer. The information on the tapes is the sole property of Amalgam Security."

Paula listened to the manager drone on about corporate policy that had been set by the CEO in White Plains. Paula shrugged and gently pushed him aside, heading to the room marked "Operations Center." The security manager looked at Dave incredulously.

"What is she doing?"

"She's ignoring you."

"She can't ignore me," he said.

"I think she just did," Dave said, amused. The manager told her to stop and went as far as to threaten her with his flashlight. Dave leaned into the manager and advised him.

"I think her gun trumps your flashlight."

The system was similar to the one at the mall, and Paula knew how to operate it. The manager continued to protest as she found the video that covered the period where Ben Curran had entered Grand Central. They saw him moving toward the trains that were heading northeast. But they couldn't zero in on which train he'd taken. It was a testament to her concentration that Paula continued reviewing the tapes while the security manager threatened legal action. Upon finishing, she and Dave left, the security manager close on their heels.

"I need your names."

"Why?" Dave asked.

"I'm writing up a report on you. This is going straight to Corporate."

Dave and Paula headed back out onto the floor, and the security manager gave up at the doorway. Luckily for them, Amalgam Security had a strict corporate policy about leaving the operations center without getting the go-ahead from Corporate in White Plains. He furrowed his brow, went back to his office, and began writing up a searing report. But he decided against it because he never obtained their names and figured that it would be better to act as though they'd never been there.

Paula's heels echoed throughout the cavernous train station. She felt a little self-conscious, but she looked good in heels. It wasn't practical for law enforcement, but taller women got more respect than shorter ones. She was five foot four, but these heels made her nearly five foot eight.

Dave and Paula found themselves walking toward the trains that were headed northeast. There were two trains rumbling quietly while a smattering of passengers boarded them.

The destinations were listed at each track. Paula looked at the names. They ranged from Boston to Westport to Providence.

"He could have gone anywhere."

"I know."

"He knew we were onto him, so he just chose to skip," Paula suggested.

"No, he killed the cell members. He didn't want them to talk. I think it was always the plan."

"Right. They obviously knew everything, so he didn't want any loose ends. He was going into the final step and didn't need them." Paula put her hands on her hips and looked out across the tracks.

"So, all we have to do is cover the states of Connecticut, Rhode Island, Massachusetts, Vermont, and New Hampshire ourselves."

"Something like that," Dave said. He sat on a wooden bench that faced track twelve. "Maybe he's meeting a contact."

"Not likely. He found a sleeper cell. They're not in contact with each other. I'm betting the heap of dead Arabs are the only one's he knew," Paula said.

Dave closed his eyes and leaned back on the bench. Nothing was coming to him. He sat up, looked at Paula, and sighed.

"He's along the Northeast Corridor somewhere."

Paula sat next to Dave. She was admittedly getting tired and needed a second wind. She complained her feet hurt her and she wished she'd worn flats. Paula looked pointedly at Dave.

"I think we ought to rent a car, drive north, and see what we can come up with," she said.

There was a map on a pillar that showed all the stops from New York to Boston. She pointed at it.

"The whole Northeast Corridor? All the way up to South Station in Boston? You are tired."

"You got a better idea?"

"Not at the moment, but I think we need something that's a little more solid."

"Maybe you're right. I am getting tired. I think I need a pick me up." Paula breezed over to a coffee stand. She bought two Red Bulls and two coffees. She made up a concoction, mixing the coffee and Red Bull, that guaranteed they'd stay wide-awake. She picked up the Red-Bull-with-coffee-chaser trick from an older agent who trained her when she was at Quantico. It was there she learned that the most valuable lessons an agent could absorb were from the seasoned field guys who'd been through a scrape or two.

She chugged her coffee/Red Bull combo. She shook after swallowing like a dog coming out of the water.

"Okay, I'm good," she pronounced.

Dave looked at his cup, leery, but started taking long sips; it began to give him his desperately needed second wind. Dave was hungry and grabbed a prepackaged sandwich out of a refrigerator case. He searched for his wallet in his jacket pocket and pulled out a small box containing twenty or so flu doses. Paula noticed it.

"What's that?"

"Huh? Oh, it's stupid. I was going to make a presentation on the flight. It was sort of a prop."

"A prop?'

"Yeah, it's how they package flu doses…"

Dave stopped looking at the tiny box that was about the size of his thumb. Paula stared at him quizzically. She nudged him to get his attention.

"Red Bull not agree with you?"

"No."

Dave opened the box and found the vial wrapped inside a thin information pamphlet. He realized that looking for what was hiding in plain sight is what made him who he was. The answer had been on him ever since he had gone to a doctor's office in Manhattan and borrowed a vial of flu doses but hadn't bothered to look at it closely.

He strained to look at the tiny print and then handed it to Paula; he couldn't read the fine print. Paula looked perplexed, unsure what he wanted her to do.

"What am I looking for?'

"Where do they make this?"

"It's in England, remember."

"No, check closer—find where it's distributed."

Paula found the name "Viral Tech" on the sheet, and its offices were located in Stamford, Connecticut. Paula looked at him and smiled.

"This has got to be it."

Dave had to be sure. He didn't know the ins and outs of how pharmaceuticals were distributed, but he knew who did. He took out his phone and dialed, then remembered the time.

"Who are you calling?" Paula asked.

"My wife."

Paula looked uncomfortable. Dave looked over to her and noticed her looking away. Dave felt self-conscious.

"Ex-wife."

It was after midnight, and the sleepy Southern voice that picked up on the other end was none too happy.

"David. Why are you calling me at this hour?" Meredith snapped.

"Look, sorry."

"Are you drunk? Are you in jail?"

"No, no, nothing like that. I'm on the job."

"What job? Emily told me they let you go."

"Don't hang up. I gotta question. It's not personal, okay?"

There was a long silence as Meredith cleared her throat. He could hear her shifting around in her bed.

"What?"

"Uh, flu doses, how many distribution centers are there?" Dave said while pacing.

"Why do you want to know that?"

"It's important," Dave said. Meredith collected herself. She knew the business backward and forward. Distribution was a key component to her customers. She had to know how quickly products could make it to them, so she made it her business to understand every part of the industry. Dave knew that she was thorough in that way. Over dinner she often filled him in on the latest discoveries she'd made.

"There's only two," she began. "Pharmfar in Stockton, California, and Viral Tech in Stamford, Connecticut. Viral Tech handles everything east of Kansas and Pharmfar handles everything west. Can I go back to sleep now?"

"Why, Kansas?"

"Lebanon, Kansas is the actual dead center of the country. Really, I'm going to sleep now."

"Thanks."

Dave hung up, and Paula stared at him tensely.

"What did she say?"

"Viral Tech in Stamford."

"Great, that's just outside New York."

The Red Bull hit Paula's system, and she was wired. Her heart was racing, and there wasn't a chance that she'd nod off.

Dave and Paula headed to the Hertz counter and rented a Yukon.

They didn't know the labyrinth of streets that made up New York City very well. They were resigned to using a street map that they found in the glove compartment. Dave was an able navigator, and after a few false starts they found themselves headed east on the Merrit Parkway into Connecticut.

Dave borrowed Paula's Blackberry and began the urgent search for directions to Viral Tech. Dave had never used a Blackberry and complained to Paula that he didn't know how to access the Internet. Paula, the ultimate multitasker, gave him a terse but succinct tutorial while speeding at eighty-five miles an hour toward Stamford.

Dave soon got the hang of the Blackberry and gave her the directions that would put them on the doorstep of Viral Tech. Dave looked at Paula, but her gaze was fixed on the highway.

"Shouldn't we call somebody?" Dave asked.

"Who? This isn't FBI sanctioned. We're Mr. Smith sanctioned, which means…"

"We're on our own."

"Did you happen to notice Smith never gave us his phone number?"

"Plausible deniability. If things collapse, he's not connected."

Dave noticed a sign that said "Stamford, 60 Miles." A trip that started out as mere busywork had developed into a national security crisis, but it would be over soon.

Dave looked at the flu-dose box, wishing that he had put two and two together sooner, but at least he finally had. He couldn't help but think of that day that seemed so long ago when he saved Lacey Paddock's life. The ability to connect the dots when they didn't seem connectable was still with him. He hadn't lost that gift. He knew he was right and could feel it down to his core. He knew what Ben Curran was going to do and how he was going to do it.

CHAPTER 34

Dave and Paula drove up to the parking lot of Viral Tech at one-thirty in the morning. The parking lot was empty. Paula pulled up and stopped at the entrance. She checked her gun and stepped out of the car. Dave leapt down from the SUV and searched for the main entrance.

The parking lot was dark, but the lights—apparently on a motion sensor system—came on as they approached the building.

Dave and Paula headed up to the large glass doors, looked inside, and saw the empty guard's desk. Paula looked for a buzzer to alert the guard, but Dave reached for the door and found it open.

They entered the lobby and walked across the thick pile rug in silence.

"Shouldn't we wait till someone's here?" Dave asked.

"There's bound to be a night guard, night janitor. Let's start looking."

Ben Curran was in the bathroom when Dave and Paula arrived so they didn't see him. But five minutes later he came out and onto the main warehouse floor.

He walked over to the surveillance station where he'd left his empty water bottle. He picked it up and was about to toss it, when he looked back at the flickering TV screens. The parking lot lights were on, which was unusual since the lights went off at night. Only someone's arrival would trigger the lights.

Ben sat at the surveillance console and turned on the camera toggle, twisting the main camera left and then right, searching the parking lot. He was beginning to wonder if it had been merely an animal crossing the motion-sensor beam, when the camera settled on the black Yukon.

Ben leapt up from the console, ran across the expansive warehouse, and reached his knapsack. He shoved items around, searching for his gun. He checked the pistol's clip, which was fully loaded. Immediately, he sprinted over to the panel that controlled the floor's lights.

Dave and Paula were still in the lobby, unsure of their next move. Dave spotted a cup of coffee on the guard's desk.

"Must be on rounds."

"Maybe he's upstairs."

Paula and Dave headed to the elevator and searched each floor for the elusive security guard. They found themselves at the door of the president of Viral Tech's office. The door was unlocked, so Dave went in, followed by Paula. He turned the light on and searched the desk. Dave slid the blotter forward and found a list of codes taped to the desk. They were listed: "Warehouse A Code, Warehouse B Code and Warehouse C Code."

"Do you believe this?"

"What?" Paula said, looking over his shoulder.

"The president of the company has the codes to all the warehouses right here. Office isn't locked, nothing."

"Works for me."

Paula copied the codes off the desk and pocketed them. They took the elevator back down and crossed to the middle of the lobby. The doors were clearly marked. The entrance to warehouse A was to the right and the nearest to them. Paula pulled out the piece of paper and punched in the code, and the door unlocked with a loud click.

"They call this secure?"

"You can't believe how many criminals I've busted by just finding out what their dogs' names were."

"I don't follow," Dave said, stepping into warehouse A.

"They put the information on computers with passwords. Some of these guys lack imagination. They use their dogs' names."

"They deserve to go to jail."

"They should give them an extra count for stupidity."

Dave and Paula entered the warehouse and began to search the floor. Dave walked up to rack seventeen and picked up one of the boxes. He put the box down and walked to rack twenty. He checked a lone box and moved through the warehouse doing random checks.

"This isn't the right warehouse."

"Why not?"

"There's no flu vaccine."

"So it must be B or C we're looking for."

Dave and Paula headed back out the door and found they needed to punch in the code to get out, just as they had to get in.

"You have to do the code and hit pound."

"I have been hitting pound."

It took Paula a few tries because the light was dimmer, and finally they heard the soft click and found themselves back in the lobby.

"Let's try B," Dave said. He took the paper with the codes and punched them in. The door opened. Paula stepped in ahead of him and surveyed the area.

Dave felt disappointed as they entered an empty warehouse. There was no product on the shelves. There was exposed wiring and the smell of fresh construction. Dave noted a mobile hook that ran the length of the ceiling. It was still wrapped in brown paper.

"Under construction."

"Damn," Paula said.

"There's still warehouse C."

"This better be it," Paula said.

Paula took the codes back from Dave and led them back out into the lobby. Paula walked to the warehouse C entrance and punched the code in. Dave and Paula entered into darkness and took a few steps.

"Where's the light switch?"

Before they found it, Ben fired four shots in their direction. They leapt to the side, landing near some boxes. The door had closed and locked behind them. Dave looked for the paper with the code printed on it, but it was lost in the darkness.

Paula whipped out her gun and then felt a burning sensation. She'd been hit. She dropped to the floor and scooted to a corner in the darkness. Dave moved toward her.

"I think he found us," Dave said.

"And he's not a bad shot."

Dave couldn't see Paula, but he reached out in the dark and examined her by touch.

Paula had been hit in the abdomen, close to the thigh. He checked for an exit wound, but there wasn't one. She was bleeding slowly. Her blouse was thin, and he tore a piece off the sleeve and worked to slow the bleeding.

Ben was as blind as they were and decided to make a rush at them. Paula heard his running footsteps and unloaded the rest of her pistol in his general direction. Ben dove to the ground and retreated down one of the leviathan-like racks. Paula switched to a fresh clip, then took out her cell phone and found she had no reception. Dave checked his and discovered the same thing. Paula winced with pain and held her side.

"That really hurts. They don't tell you that when you fill out the job application."

"You're going to be okay."

"If I get to a hospital." Dave didn't answer.

"There's gotta be a phone in here. I'm gonna call 911."

Dave stood and crept away from Paula. His choice of clothing turned out to be fortuitous. He was wearing all black, and he could barely be seen in the darkness.

He moved with stealth, not wanting to draw Ben's attention. A voice called out from a distant corner.

"Who are you?" Ben Curran called. Dave didn't answer.

"I know I hit her."

Dave stopped when he saw what looked like a faint light on a desk. He hoped it was a phone, but as he got closer he realized it was merely a server to a computer setup.

"You don't know who you're dealing with," Ben went on. "I'm pretty good at this." Dave moved along a rack and accidentally knocked a box off of it. He heard Ben running for him, and Dave leapt and rolled quietly, moving to a different aisle.

He heard the footsteps stop. He thought he'd go back the way he came in, but he didn't remember the code to get out. Ben would kill him if he even went near the door. Dave crept along the rack, not making a sound.

"What was your training? Navy Seals? Marines? What?" Ben's voice queried. Dave remembered his Wing Chun training in Atlanta. It was about close combat. In the last few classes he had to master fighting blindfolded. He hoped it would be money well spent.

Dave reached the end of rack nine. He peeked around and saw a table but no phone. He looked to his right and found a pair of large scissors. It was better than nothing.

"Well, look, I can't chase you all night, but I've good idea where your friend is. Maybe I'll finish the job."

Dave stopped. He knew Ben was baiting him, but he also knew that Ben Curran wouldn't hesitate to kill Paula. Paula still had her gun, and Dave hoped he'd minimized her blood loss.

Dave turned and stealthily moved back up rack eight. In class, he had faced the test of defending himself in total darkness. Then, it had been merely a game. It was something to help him focus his mind. He never imagined he might have to use these skills in a life-and-death situation.

Ben listened intently for any movement, but Dave's precision frustrated him. He assumed he was dealing with a pro. Ben decided to head back toward Paula. He needed to kill both of them so he could get away with a solid head start.

Ben quietly moved up toward the entrance and heard labored breathing. He smiled, knowing he would have his target in his sights soon.

Ben followed the sound of the short gasps, moving in for the kill. There was a red exit light that didn't offer much illumination, but he could see Paula's foot bathed in the red light. He moved through the darkness to line up his shot.

What he didn't know was that Dr. Dave Richards was standing between him and Paula. In announcing his target, he'd made a grave mistake and had given Dave the advantage. Dave knew where Ben was going, and Ben couldn't see Dave.

Dave stood perfectly still as Ben eased toward Paula, and Ben passed within a foot of him. Dave raised his arm. Ben felt the oddest feeling. Something had plunged into his neck. He reached around and felt something metal. Dave was only inches away from him.

Dave had stuck a pair of scissors into his neck, punching right through his carotid artery and his windpipe. Ben stumbled backward.

Ben dropped his gun, and it clattered to the ground. He reached for the scissors and pulled them out, but it was too late. He fell back, slamming the back of his head on the cement floor.

Ben's last thought was that they had sent the crème de la crème to get him. At least it wasn't some poorly trained ATF agent. They had sent the best. Ben hoped his dad would be proud of him when they were finally together again. It would be soon.

When Dave heard that familiar final throaty exhale he had heard too many times before in his residency, he knew that Ben was dead. By the time he found Paula, she was unconscious. Time was of the essence. He found her gun and fired it into the door until the lock gave way.

Dave carried Paula into the lobby, cradling her tightly. He reached for the phone at the guard's desk and dialed 911.

CHAPTER 35

Dave lifted Paula into the ambulance. She was unconscious. He was about to board the ambulance when the local police officer pulled him aside.

"We've got some questions, Doctor."

"I really need to be with her," Dave said.

"We'll get you there soon enough. We need to know what happened here."

Reluctantly, Dave got out of the ambulance, and it headed off to Stamford Hospital without him.

A sergeant looked at Dave and pointed back at warehouse C.

"You mind telling me who shot the FBI agent?"

"The dead guy."

"The agent killed him?"

"I did."

"Uh, okay, so you shot him?"

"Cut an artery in his neck he really needed. Look, Sergeant, I need to get back in there."

"Wait a minute. I got some more questions."

"His name's Ben Curran. ATF's been after him for a while. Now I got to do my job."

"Why were you after him?"

"Look, I gotta wrap things up in there. So if you wanna follow me, be my guest. I don't have time for twenty questions."

Dave looked at his watch. It was six a.m., and the sun was just beginning to peek over the horizon. A Jeep Wagoneer drove into the lot and parked crookedly. A man jumped out of his SUV, carrying a bag of muffins in one hand and a large cup of coffee in the other, and approached Dave.

"What the hell's going on here?" the man asked.

"You work here?" Dave asked.

"I'm Hoyt Mulvehill, distribution supervisor."

"Warehouse C?"

"Yes."

"I'm Dr. Dave Richards from the CDC."

"CDC?"

"I need your help."

"Dr. Richards, I'm not done," the sergeant said.

"Well, I am."

Dave ushered Hoyt into warehouse C. When Hoyt saw the coroner examining Ben Curran's body, he fell into a nearby swivel chair. He dropped his coffee, and it spilled on the concrete floor.

"So what was he going to do?" Hoyt asked.

"Infect the flu-dose supply."

"Good Christ. Good Christ."

"Take it easy."

"You don't understand. He was asking a lot of questions," Hoyt said.

"About what?"

"He wanted to know how distribution worked. He wanted to know which shipments were going to which cities."

"Specific cities?"

"Yeah. He said his grandmother was in Boca and was curious which boxes were headed that way. See, it's all organized by region and city."

Hoyt pointed to the aisle upon aisle of flu-dose cartons. Dave looked at Hoyt.

"I'm pretty sure Ben's grandmother is long dead." Dave looked around the warehouse warily.

"Did he ask you about any other areas?" Dave asked.

"Other areas?"

"Yeah, did he ask about other cities?"

"Yeah, uh, Detroit and Houston."

"Detroit and Houston? When was that?"

"I dunno, he was always asking me something about how I did my job. I thought he was angling for a promotion or something."

"When was the last time you delivered to those cities?"

"Are you kidding? It's flu season; we're delivering every day."

Dave flashed on something. When Smith showed him and Paula the picture of Ben going into Grand Central, he had something under his arm. Dave wished he could look at it again. Dave began searching the vast racks that covered the warehouse floor. Hoyt followed after him closely. A muscle-bound black cop who had been searching Ben's body for evidence began to listen in.

"What are you looking for?' Hoyt asked.

"A box. I think he brought a box in with him. You ever see him carrying a small carton?"

"No, never. He'd get here before me. He worked the night shift."

"There a break room here?"

"No."

"Do the employees on the floor have uniforms?

"Sure."

"Where do they change?"

"The locker room."

"Show me?"

Dave and the cop followed Hoyt over to a locker room. It was dingy and smelled of body odor. The lockers were old and gray and scratched up. There was a long wooden bench that ran the length of the room.

Dave stepped ahead of Hoyt and walked along the lockers looking at the names. Each locker was assigned to an employee, and a thin cloth tape was stuck to each one with a name written in Sharpie. Dave looked at every locker carefully, but Ben's name wasn't there.

"Wait a minute. What name did he go by?" Dave asked.

The cop, who was standing nearby, stepped forward.

"The nameplate on the body said Jones."

Dave looked down the lockers and saw the one at the very end marked "Jones." He jumped over a bench and stopped in front of the locker. It was padlocked.

"You guys got any bolt cutters?"

"Yeah, I think so."

Hoyt went to the other end of the locker room and opened a door to a storage closet. He flipped on the light, but the bulb was burned out.

"Dammit. Can you help me out here?"

The cop whipped out his flashlight and lit up the small room. Dave heard Hoyt cursing as loose objects fell around him.

"I got it."

Hoyt emerged from the locker room with a large bolt cutter. The cop grabbed it away from him.

"Be faster if I do it," the cop said. The cop hustled to the locker and lined up the bolt cutter. He snapped the lock off in an instant. Dave moved in and opened the locker and saw the gray box sitting at the bottom.

It was opened. He checked for how many vials remained. Many of the boxes were empty. Dave looked at Hoyt and the cop.

"What the hell is this?" Hoyt said, recoiling from the box.

"Rabies. And it looks like we're too late."

Dave sat on the wooden bench. Paula's coffee and Red Bull concoction was wearing off, and he needed a second wind. Hoyt sat next to him.

"My God. And he sent them to Houston, Detroit, and Boca. Why those cities?"

That had been gnawing at Dave. He couldn't immediately figure out the significance. But Ben was a dark, calculating character with a clear agenda. Dave paused in thought. He had put it all together. He shook his head in disgust.

"What?" Hoyt said.

"Sick bastard. Boca Raton has a large population of Jews, Houston has a huge Hispanic population, and Detroit has an 80 percent African American population."

"Why would he do that?' Hoyt asked.

"He's a white supremacist. He's going after everybody he hates."

"I didn't know what he was up to," Hoyt said.

"Look, I need your records. I need to know where this stuff was shipped. Hospitals, doctor's offices, everything."

Hoyt moved quickly out of the locker room. They followed him across the warehouse floor over to Hoyt's computer station where he began typing away, trying to find out what kind of damage Ben had done.

Hoyt typed up the schedule, and it began to print out on a nearby printer.

"I only need the last four days," Dave said.

Hoyt looked through the sheets of printout and tore out a section. He handed them to Dave, who looked it over, biting his lower lip.

"At least five thousand boxes were shipped," Dave said, looking at the list.

"Like I told you, it's our high season."

"He couldn't have infected all of them. He had three night shifts."

"Hell, he had all day. He could have been doing them at home, too. He was guarding this stuff. He could have taken a carload with him. We'd never know. And he knew exactly when each carton was being shipped out."

Dave tried to estimate how many vials you could infect in an hour. Ben must have been injecting the rabies into the doses with a tiny needle. Dave looked at Hoyt.

"How long does it take from shipment to delivery?"

"It's all overnight."

"So everything that went out yesterday..."

"Will be received in the next few hours," Hoyt said.

Dave knew he had a weighty decision to make. If he didn't let the public know the gravity of the crisis, countless more Americans could be infected by lunchtime.

Smith had been wrong. It didn't turn out to be in his and Paula's hands; it had fallen solely into his. He had to make a decision that could cause a panic. If he called Lussier, he'd order a study group and waste time while more people were infected.

Dave walked out of Viral Tech. It was sunny and cool. He sat on a bench and picked up his phone. He thought about calling Dr. Root but decided he couldn't involve him. He had a wife and a kid, and he couldn't expose him to the kind of fire he was about to be exposed to. Dave didn't have Smith's number, and it didn't matter. Smith got what he wanted; he orchestrated the elimination of the White Sleeper.

Dave looked through his phone log and saw a number he couldn't recall. Then he looked at the area code and realized it was Channing Zumwalt's cell phone. Zumwalt had called him to clarify some information for the president. It was a brief call, and Dave quickly forgot about it.

Dave hit the send button, and the phone rang; Channing answered the phone.

"Zumwalt."

"Sir, its Dr. Richards."

"Yes, Dr. Richards. Do you have good news?"

"We caught him. He's dead."

"Excellent. Good work."

"Don't congratulate me yet. He was well in process of sending out the virus."

"Good God. Where'd he send it?"

"Principally, he was targeting black, Hispanic, and Jewish population centers: Boca, Houston, and Detroit. But he had enough time to hit more than just those three cities."

"How bad is it? Any clue as to how many victims?"

"No, it could be ten thousand. It could be a hundred. Each dose has ten injections in it."

There was a long silence on the other end. Dave let the news sink in before continuing.

"There's time, but I'm going to have to do something you may not approve of and I'll accept the consequences."

"What do you have to do?" Zumwalt said.

"I have to go on television and tell everyone to stop taking flu shots. That the shots have been compromised."

"I think we better discuss this."

"There's no time. This is a courtesy call only," Dave said.

"Dr. Richards, you could create a panic. I need to discuss this with the president."

"I understand, but time's too critical. The next set of tainted vials are arriving at doctor's offices as we speak. I just wanted you to know that what I am doing is out of necessity."

"This isn't your decision, Dr. Richards."

"It has to be. Your agenda's complex; mine's simple. I have to save lives and that's what I'm going to do. I'm getting off the phone before you convince me otherwise." Dave hung up. His cell began ringing. It was Zumwalt. He pocketed the phone.

Dave looked up and saw a TV truck rounding the corner. It stopped, and a young blonde reporter flung the passenger door open. Dave was a little surprised. Her suit looked as though she'd slept in it. She asked a cop on the scene a question that Dave couldn't hear. The cop pointed at Dave, and she ran toward him, nearly stumbling on her high heels. She pulled out a notepad. A cameraman slid in behind her.

"I understand there was a shooting and a death. Could you fill me in?" she said in her youthful voice.

Dave thought about destiny as he looked into her eyes. This girl didn't know it, but she was about to be broadcasting her story nationally. She probably had never dreamed that she'd handle the big story. She was obviously the cute reporter assigned fluff pieces, but all that was about to change

"The flu-dose supply has been compromised. It is critical that in the cities of Boca Raton, Houston, and Detroit flu shots must cease immediately. Anyone who has received a flu shot in the last four days needs to be checked for rabies exposure."

Miranda Cooper lost her train of thought and looked back at the cameraman in disbelief. Miranda looked back at Dave.

"What do you mean?" Miranda asked. "Doctor, are you saying that people have been taking flu shots tainted with rabies?"

"That's exactly what I'm saying."

"How did this happen?"

"I can't get into the details as of yet, but I'd suggest that anyone east of Kansas who's had a flu shot needs to be checked for rabies exposure. Now at this early stage this is very treatable. "

Miranda almost froze when she heard this but pressed ahead like a pro.

Miranda was a bright girl who stepped up to the plate and asked all the right questions. She finished taping and told her cameraman to uplink the story to the station ASAP.

Dave sat on the curb as a radio reporter shoved a microphone in his face. Dave gave the same story, and the reporter raced off to get his story out, too.

The news spread like wildfire. It was soon the lead story on the cable news channels. By noon, flu vials were isolated to be checked for viral contamination and hospitals and doctor's offices were jammed with panicked Americans, desperate to be checked for exposure.

Dr. Root found out about the extent of the exposure when everyone else did. He knew he had to marshal his forces to gather enough of the rabies vaccine to deal with the problem. Most ERs only carried around twenty doses at a time. Root had his staff drop everything and find every last vial.

They searched all over the country and the rest of the world to deal with this panic. Root used his connections in Washington to talk to leaders from the United Kingdom to China.

Miraculously, the world responded, and the medicine made its way to Atlanta and out to the parts of the country it needed to reach.

CHAPTER 36

Dr. Lussier was having lunch in the Claridge House in London. He was having kippers and eggs, not because he liked them but because he felt it was the thing to do when in the United Kingdom. He sipped some coffee and was joined by Agent Pearson. His characteristic stoicism was gone as he marched up to Lussier. Pearson was carrying a phone and handed it to him.

"It's the president."

Lussier stuttered in disbelief. He slowly took the phone, hoping it was a prank, and when he heard the distinctive voice on the other end he knew it wasn't. The president wanted to know what was going on with the White Sleeper situation. Lussier got puffed up and said, "Well, Mr. President, I'm on his trail in London, and I'm confident we'll have him soon."

There was a long silence, and then the president said, "What the hell are you doing in England?"

"Uh, the White Sleeper. I'm here with…uh…Director Russell."

"They caught him in Stamford, Connecticut, a few hours ago. We got a huge recall of flu doses going on. Why the hell don't you know that?"

The president hung up; Pearson took back the phone and walked away, joining Director Russell, who conferred with Pearson while looking over at Lussier.

Lussier made his way up to his room, turned on the TV, and saw Dr. Dave Richard's face on CNN, Fox, and the BBC. Lussier sat on the edge of the bed in utter despair. The phone rang, and it was an FBI underling saying that they were flying back to New York within the hour.

Dr. Lussier hadn't unpacked, so he checked out of Claridge's and found himself being transported to the airport alone. Director Russell and the rest of the FBI entourage went in a separate car.

The weather was typically foggy, and their plane left midday to go back across the Atlantic. Lussier didn't speak to anyone as he tried to calculate how he was going to turn this in his favor. The CDC had been instrumental in catching the White Sleeper, and he was the head of Counterterrorism. But as he lay in his chair on the FBI jet traveling at forty thousand feet above the Earth, the chess pieces of his career were being moved.

Channing Zumwalt was getting an earful from the president. He wanted to know why the director of counterterrorism at the CDC was clearly out of the loop. He asked for Lussier's file and asked Zumwalt to find out more information on him. Zumwalt rushed out of the Oval Office and to the chief of staff's nearby desk. The chief of staff was at a press briefing, so he commandeered his desk and phone.

Zumwalt made a series of well-placed calls about Lussier, and the consensus was that Dr. Evan Lussier was nothing more than a mediocre civil servant.

Zumwalt's last call was to a man who seemed to have his finger in everything. He knew him as only Mr. Smith, but he could always get a hold of him. He'd heard he'd consulted on the case and wanted to know what he thought of Dr. Lussier.

"Lussier? Oh, yes, I know him. CDC."

"What's your take on him?"

"I don't like to talk out of school. Seems pleasant enough. A C-lister in an A-list position. But that's the way of government, isn't it?"

Channing didn't know what to make of that statement. Smith seemed indifferent.

"And of course his affair with his assistant is rather scandalous. Bound to come out. His wife does fund-raising, salt of the Earth."

Smith was obviously recommending Lussier's removal. A CIA operative couldn't care less about the morality of a man cheating on his wife unless he wanted to use it against him. Channing also learned that Smith had given Dr. Richards a gentle push in the direction he followed to conclude the case. Channing knew he had to relate that to the president. The president was a fan of the CIA and less so the FBI. The FBI had at times investigated the president's past business dealings, whereas the CIA couldn't have cared less.

By the time Dr. Lussier was a third of the way across the Atlantic, Channing Zumwalt was having a meeting with the chief of staff, Ken Folsom. Ken listened intently to the national security advisor.

By the time Dr. Lussier was at the halfway point in his flight to New York, the chief of staff had called a meeting with the vice president's office and the press secretary to discuss Dr. Evan Lussier.

By the time Dr. Lussier's plane was on approach to JFK, the president was being briefed on Dr. Lussier. They gave him less than a glowing report. The general feeling was he was out of his league. The president wasn't sure if it was worth making a change until Zumwalt mentioned Lussier's alleged indiscretions.

The president looked over his glasses and said, "I think Dr. Lussier needs to spend more time with his family."

Zumwalt added that there was bound to be a public outcry that the flu-dose supply had been used as a weapon, and someone had to take responsibility. The president smiled and said that they'll have Dr. Lussier to blame. The director of White House communications would make sure of that.

When Dr. Lussier's plane touched down at Kennedy, he stepped off the plane and found someone tapping his shoulder. It was Pearson again. He gave him a phone and learned he was being summoned to Washington, DC.

Lussier prepared for a presentation that he would never make. He thought it odd that he was told to go to an unknown building off K Street. He was made to wait for an extended period of time. This rankled Lussier.

He was brought in to see Samuel Dodd. Dodd was a junior deputy national security advisor who'd only graduated from Georgetown two years ago. He was twenty-five and looked like a freshman Lussier had hazed back in college many years ago.

Lussier sat down, checking his files, and Dodd smiled.

"I took the liberty of making some notes that we can pursue with regards to the White Sleeper case. Is Channing going to be here?"

"Mr. Zumwalt? No, no, he won't be."

"Homeland Security? We really saved the day, but I don't think we can rest on our laurels, if you know what I mean. I think we need to take three critical approaches in the future…"

"You won't need that."

"Excuse me?" Lussier pushed his glasses back up his nose.

"You don't have to show me any reports or anything. That's not what this is about."

"Then what is it about?"

"In light of the events, I've been advised to advise you that your services are no longer required."

Lussier stuttered and sat back, stunned.

"What do you mean?"

"You are no longer the director of counterterrorism at the CDC. We've prepared various resignation letters for your perusal. I like the one about wanting to spend more time with your family."

"Who the hell are you that you're telling me this?" Lussier said.

"Well, frankly, sir, I'm quite low in the pecking order, which will give you some idea of how well you're regarded."

"Who ordered this?"

"The president. You can to take it up with him if you have a problem with it."

Dodd offered an envelope with the letters of resignation. Lussier took the letters as his eyes filled with rage.

"So I guess we're clear." Dodd rose and offered his hand. Lussier didn't respond.

"Well, I have a lunch meeting at the Old Ebbitt Grill. Good luck, Dr. Lussier."

With that, Dodd left the office before Lussier was able to say another word.

CHAPTER 37

While Dr. Evan Lussier's career was coming to an end in an office on K Street, Dr. Root was fielding calls from the press about the White Sleeper incident. His secretary Cory walked into his office and told him he had a call from Washington, DC.

Root picked up the phone.

"Root."

"Neil Zinner, deputy chief of staff to the vice president."

"Hi, Neil."

"Listen, we're all thrilled that you had the foresight to assign Dr. Richards to the White Sleeper case."

"Well, Dr. Richards is quite valued around here."

"Good. We wanted to feel you out about something."

"Sure. What is it?"

"We'd like to know if you'd take the director's position in your department."

"Excuse me?"

"We'd like you to be the director of counterterrorism in the CDC."

"What about Dr. Lussier?"

"We needed to make a change. Will you take the job?"

"Yes, of course."

"Thank you."

Dr. Root hung up and sat back in his chair. Dr. Dave Richards had improved his life again. Dave had inadvertently lined up the position Root had never imagined he would get. Now he was in the driver's seat. He looked at his phone, paused, and then picked it up to call Dave. It rang several times before Dave answered.

"Hi," Dave said tentatively.

"Guess you've been busy."

"You calling to tear my head off?"

"Hardly. I need you back down here."

"Doubt Lussier feels the same way." There was a long pause that Dave couldn't quite understand.

Dr. Root cleared his throat and said modestly, "I'm the new Lussier."

CHAPTER 38

Dave didn't know anything about the reputation of Stamford Hospital. But he had asked around and learned the care was highly regarded. This put him at ease. He hated playing the role of the doctor, micromanaging a friend's care, when the staff was underperforming.

"I'm looking for Paula Mushari."

The admitting nurse looked up her room and then said, "Room 320 East."

Dave felt at home in the halls of a hospital. He had been out of his element for awhile, and now he happily absorbed the familiar sterile smell. Dave entered room 320 East and found Paula hooked up to an IV. She had a *Star* magazine lying at her side. Dave took her chart and flipped it open.

"They gave you the good stuff," he said.

"They could shoot me again, and I wouldn't feel a thing," Paula said.

Dave leaned in and gave her a kiss on the forehead. She frowned. Dave noticed.

"What's wrong?"

"You missed." Paula pointed toward her lips. Dave looked to see if anyone was watching and then gave her a gentle kiss. He backed up and rested his hand on her thigh.

"We got the bad guy," Paula said, smiling.

"Got half the country freaked out."

"That's what the CDC is supposed to do. You get your job back?"

"Yeah, my buddy's in charge now."

"What happened to Lussier?"

"Axed, I guess. Nobody said."

"So you're going back to Atlanta?"

"Yeah, tonight. Gotta move my stuff to the corner office."

Paula told him to sit on the bed. She gently took his hand.

"You made your own destiny. I told you."

"Well, you seem to be right about a lot of things."

"They taught me well in Quantico."

"I suspect you taught them."

"So, Dr. Richards. What are we going to do?"

"To do?" Dave said.

"About us?"

Dave smiled warmly and reached out for her when Director Russell appeared at the door and boldly entered, flashing his trademark insincere grin.

"There's our girl." Russell shook her weak hand.

"How are you feeling?"

"Little groggy, sir."

"You take all the time you need because we're going to need your expertise in New York. Transferring to my department suits you, I assume?"

Paula looked at Dave, surprised. She tried to sit up but winced from the pain.

"Yes, sir. Of course, sir."

"We'll catch up later," Dave said.

"Right, sure, Doctor. Sure," Paula said.

Dave excused himself and stood outside the door. He could hear Director Russell.

"Now, Agent Mushari. It would be helpful if it were understood that I had sanctioned your investigation at Viral Tech. This of course is to protect you."

"Oh, yes sir. I understand. You wanted to have a backup plan."

"That's right. Very good. We don't want a Lussier situation now, do we?"

"No sir."

"You see, Paula, this business runs on credit, and we've got this one. Of course Dr. Richards shares in that glory, but we've got our juicy piece of it."

Dave looked in the room. Paula looked awkwardly at him. Dave gave her a knowing wink, and she smiled. Russell looked around, but Dave had already turned away from the door.

Dave took the elevator and found Mr. Smith waiting inside. Smith urged him to come on board by curling his bony hand toward himself. Smith wiped his hands with a napkin. Dave nervously stepped in, and the doors closed.

"How's she doing?" Smith asked.

"Fine. She's going to be fine."

"Good. I can always spot talent, and you two are the real articles."

"Thank you."

"Too bad about Lussier."

Dave couldn't help but think that the news had traveled fast—almost too fast. The elevator doors opened, and Smith wandered out and winked at Dave.

"You can thank me later."

Smith slipped away into a crowd of people. Dave realized that he'd picked up a benefactor. Smith probably had been instrumental in saving his job. But benefactors often want to collect on the things you presume are gifts but turn out to be debts.

As Dave stepped out of Stamford Hospital, the first thing he noticed was the snowflakes falling in the parking lot. The cloud cover had come in quickly. He smiled. He'd been in Atlanta so long he'd missed several winters. He was delighted to see the steady white stream start to dust the pavement beneath his feet. A gaggle of reporters accosted him, spitting out a cacophony of questions. Too many and too fast, he couldn't distinguish one from another. He brushed by them when he saw a familiar face. It was Agent Pearson. He managed a smile, the first one since Dave had met him. Pearson stood in the growing storm, his hands folded before him, unaffected by the weather. Dave walked over, the press tailing him tightly.

"You look like a man who needs a ride," Pearson said. "Director Root asked us to get you home ASAP."

"But Agent Mushari…"

"I'll make your apologies."

Pearson pulled his sleeve up to his lips and quietly spoke into a mic that was out of Dave's view. Pearson nodded and listened, and then a black Crown Victoria came up and stopped in front of them. Dave stepped into the backseat of the car.

Pearson closed the door, and the car sped off as the photographers tried desperately to grab a final picture of Dr. Dave Richards. The car headed directly to JFK, and he was on his way back to Atlanta by mid-afternoon.

CHAPTER 39

Dave didn't go directly to the CDC when he arrived in Atlanta. He went home for a change of clothes and a shower in his meager apartment. His cell phone had racked up a pile of messages, but he felt a deep need to relax. He wasn't trained to be an action hero, but circumstances had forced him into it. It wasn't that he wasn't fit. But chasing after a maniac bent on killing hundreds of thousands of people would be enough to exhaust anyone.

When he got back to his place, he played his messages and heard both his mother and father telling him how proud they were of him. His brother had even called from Calcutta where he was working on an irrigation project. Dave couldn't believe the story had reached that far around the world.

He lay on the couch but didn't turn on the TV. He didn't need to see the story reported over and over. He'd lived it.

It was three in the afternoon. Dave needed to check in with the office and maybe ask Dr. Root for some time off.

Dave entered the CDC and immediately felt he was in an alternate universe. Total strangers rushed up to him, pumping his hands in congratulations. There was no more whispering behind his back. He had strived for and received redemption.

He shrugged it off and headed down to his basement office and found it empty. A file clerk who was using the rarely used basement bathroom asked him why he was in the dungeon.

"My office was here."

"They moved you up to the top floor. You got Dr. Root's old office."

Dave didn't react. He headed back up the stairs and took the elevator to the top floor. Dr. Root had wasted no time in taking control of counterterrorism.

Dave approached his new office, a corner office with a view of the forest behind the building. The winter had stripped the magnolia trees of their blossoms, but that didn't make Dave enjoy the view any less.

"Take good care of it," Dr. Root said, coming up behind Dave. Dave spun around and, seeing Dr. Root, gave him an uncharacteristic hug.

"Good job. What else can I say?" Dr. Root said.

"Thanks for this."

"There's also a salary bump. You're getting my old job."

"You're kidding."

"Nope, well, what do you expect? You saved countless lives."

"So what's the latest?"

"We're tracking down everyone who was infected. Looks like we caught it in time."

"How many?"

"Rough estimates are he infected maybe ten thousand. We're basically giving everyone the rabies series who got injections from the Viral Tech lot last week. We're destroying the Stamford supply and have the UK working 24-7 to make up the shortfall. The western distributor wasn't compromised, so we're working with them to keep the flu-dose supply up and running."

"Good," said Dave as he sat in his new chair.

"I'm sorry," Dr. Root said, sitting on the leather couch.

"Sorry about what?"

"Firing you."

"It wasn't you. You're my best friend in the world. I know you did everything you could."

Dr. Root felt the same way, but it wasn't something men typically declared to each other; they simply were best friends or they weren't.

"I need some time off," Dave said.

"I know, but we've got a mother of a report to write first. And we've got to go up to DC for a briefing tomorrow."

"I need to get you up to speed."

"Not me. You. You're the star of the hour. Everybody wants to hear the story from the horse's mouth."

"Right."

"Glad I sent you on that little errand. It paid off."

Dave agreed. His world had been falling apart, and now it was coming back together. And it was all due to a crazed young man named Ben Curran—a man destined for failure. And if Ben were destined for failure, perhaps that meant Dave was destined for success. It was hard for him to think that way. Success had been so elusive for so long he could barely remember what it tasted like. But he was reminded soon enough by the constant calls that day. He was invited to speak at numerous functions. He had so many offers that an agency called him about representing him on speaking tours. Dave declined the offer. A publisher inquired about a book. He didn't mind brief fame, but extended attention had no appeal for him. He wanted to do what he did best.

Dave and Dr. Root went to Washington and spoke to various subcommittees on the subject of securing the flu-dose supply. They would be put on a panel of former senators, secretaries of defense, and directors of state and federal health and human services.

Eventually, this panel would generate a thick report that the nation's drug supply was sorely in need of securing from further terrorist action. The CDC was charged with implementing these guidelines.

All employees of critical drug distribution centers now had to go through rigorous background checks. The ease with which Ben Curran decimated the flu-dose supply would not be possible again.

Viral Tech's stock value dropped from twenty dollars a share on the Nasdaq down to five dollars. It became an opportunity for Merck to scoop up the company and make major changes to the culture of Viral Tech.

The winners were obvious: the CDC, the FBI, and in the quietest of quarters in documents marked "Top Secret," there was detailed information that bragged that the CIA's involvement ultimately saved the day.

This, of course, set well with the president, and he chose to look the other way in terms of any unofficial official CIA domestic actions. This made Mr. Smith a very happy man.

As Dave headed out of the Senate subcommittee meeting in the Senate building, he saw Smith one more time.

Dave and Dr. Root were invited to eat in the Senate dining room, and Mr. Smith was having lunch with a congressman on the intelligence committee. Smith merely winked at Dave, and Dave gave Smith a nod. Dr. Root noticed the exchange.

"Who was that?"

"Guy I met in New York."

"Doesn't look familiar. Who is he?"

"To be absolutely honest, I have no idea. But I suspect he's the reason that we're sitting here today."

Dave's cell phone had been ringing incessantly for days. Mostly, he ignored it. He just let it sit on the table until the caller gave up. But this time he looked down, and the phone number was familiar. It was Meredith.

CHAPTER 40

Dave walked up to his old house and hit the doorbell. The lawn was perfectly manicured. Meredith answered the door and gave him a warm smile. She looked startlingly beautiful in her tight jeans and simple white top. Her hair had been recently done in a flip, and her makeup was applied with such perfection it was hard to tell she was wearing any.

"Lawn looks great," Dave said.

"Hi, David," she said sweetly in her ladylike Southern drawl.

"Hi. Sorry I woke you up the other day."

"You had to. Obviously. Come on in."

She walked in, and he took in her panther-like gait as he followed her. He couldn't help but wonder why she'd called him. She hadn't tried to contact him since they'd separated. He saw a thick packet of papers with a legal firm's name on it on the table in the foyer. It was the divorce papers he hadn't signed yet.

Meredith had tea set up in the breezeway. They sat on some dark green metal chairs. Meredith poured the tea. Dave took his cup and had a sip.

"So, tell me the truth. Are you okay?" Meredith asked.

"I'm fine. Nothing broken. Just some bruises."

She wanted to know the blow-by-blow of how the White Sleeper case had unfolded. Dave filled her in on the intrigue of the last few weeks, and she listened with rapt attention.

Every time he tried to tell her about how much he had changed, she asked about a detail that Dave had skipped over. She was amazed by his exploits, especially when he told her about trying to save the terrorist from drowning.

"Did you feel conflicted?"

"Conflicted how?"

"I mean, he had tried to kill you."

"Well, we certainly could have used the information he had, but that didn't pan out, of course."

"So tell me, David. This must have been awfully stressful for you."

"More than you could imagine."

"Did you succumb?"

Dave didn't know what she meant. At first he thought she was referring to Paula, but then realized she was asking about his alcoholism. She hadn't asked about that in awhile.

"No, no, I didn't. That's in the past, Meredith."

Meredith smiled at him in a way she hadn't in years. Dave was heartened.

Meredith looked at her watch. She rose in her elegant way.

"I'm late for a meeting with some of my girlfriends." She put her arm through his and walked him toward the door.

"Let's catch up over dinner tomorrow."

Dave didn't want to appear to be eager and coolly said, "I can't. I got to help a friend."

"Really? Maybe later."

"I might be gone for a week. I'll call you when I get back."

She walked him out to his car with her arm still tucked in his.

"Did you hear the scandal about Dr. Lussier? I understand that his assistant Maureen and he were having big goings-on, if you know what I mean, and at the Omni of all places. Can't fire her of course. Too many legal ramifications."

"You're kidding."

"Emily Root told me the whole sordid tale," she said. Dave shook his head.

"I can't imagine anyone wanting to see Lussier naked," Dave said wryly.

Meredith burst out laughing in a way he hadn't seen in years. Dave opened his car door, and she kissed him on the cheek.

"You just make sure that they don't assign that Maureen to your office."

"Very funny."

CHAPTER 41

Paula Mushari was packing up her apartment. She had accumulated so much in the last four years; the boxes never seemed to end. She considered tossing everything and starting over, but that wasn't a reasonable option. New York was pricey, and her salary bump wasn't big enough for her to be cavalier.

It was late in the afternoon when she finally decided to take a break. She flopped down on the couch. The doorbell rang, and she grumbled. Her neighbors had been bothering her since the White Sleeper story had broken. They discovered she was an FBI agent, and they now bothered her with every minor dispute that popped up in the neighborhood.

She hauled herself up, went to the door, opened it, and found Dave standing there holding a roll of packing tape.

"Need any help?"

Paula pulled him in and kissed him. He kissed her back. She held onto him for the longest time.

"What are you doing here?"

"I had vacation time coming. Figured I'd help you move."

"I was dreading this until you showed up." Paula sat on the couch and Dave sat with her. "So, you never answered my question in the hospital."

"Which one was that?"

"The us thing."

"I live in Atlanta, Paula."

"I'm going to live in New York," she said.

"But I have to be in DC at least once a week."

"So do I," Paula said, nuzzling him.

"Things worked out, didn't they?"

"Yeah. Just keep your eyes open."

"What do you mean?"

"When you're successful, it can open a Pandora's box. A lot of eyes are going to be on you. You have to choose your friends carefully."

"Like the Mr. Smiths and the CIA?"

"No, I'm not talking about him. If you can believe it, he's probably one of the good guys."

"What people?"

"Let's not worry about that. We deserve some time off."

Paula looked at Dave and realized he was still in many ways an innocent. She held him tighter, realizing that she might need to protect him in the future. As she looked into his eyes, she knew their destinies were intertwined.